A Great British Video Nasty Nightmare

Harrison Phillips

For Mom and Dad –

Thank you for letting the TV raise me…

It messed me up just the right amount.

FOREWORD

During the late 1970s, as home video recorders became more easily accessible to the general public, concerns were raised about the possibility of young children gaining access to material that was deemed to be excessively violent.

In the early 1980s, the Director of Public Prosecutions released a list of 72 movies which they believed may be in violation of Section 2 of the 'Obscene Publications Act 1959' – meaning that certain scenes within those films may be liable to cause severe mental harm to anybody who may view them (particularly children). It was these movies – mostly, low-budget horror movies – that became known colloquially as the "Video Nasties". Of these 72 movies, 39 were successfully prosecuted, making their distribution illegal, punishable by up to 10 years imprisonment, as well as a £10,000 fine. The remaining 33, although not prosecuted, were still either refused certification by the British Board of Film Classification (as per the Video Recordings Act 1984), or they were not submitted to the BBFC for certification. This, effectively, made it illegal to supply these films also. Many movies fell afoul of the censors during this period, including such well-known titles as I Spit On Your Grave, Last House On The Left, Faces Of Death, Cannibal Holocaust and The Evil Dead.

During this time, a number of high-profile politicians, morality campaigners, and tabloid journalists pushed the idea that these movies posed a serious threat to the wellbeing of the nation's children. It was assumed that watching violence in movies would somehow lead to real-life acts of violence. Although the idea was, for the most part, laughable. One politician even went so far as to suggest that the "Video Nasties" may even cause harm to dogs… It was this insistence that led to the majority of these videos being confiscated and destroyed, and the introduction of new laws to govern the burgeoning home video industry.

It has never been proven whether or not any of the claims made were justified. No link has ever been proven between violence on video, and violence in real life…

The Great British Video Nasty Nightmare

Oakhill, England

October 1984

Chapter One:

Home Sweet Home

No matter how many times Amy flipped through the channels, there was always nothing to watch. The news was playing on BBC1; nothing of any interest had happened in the past twenty-four hours to make paying any attention even worthwhile. BBC2 was playing some old Western starring Clint Eastwood, not something that Amy – nor Tina, for that matter – would be interested in watching. *The Bill* was currently on ITV. Amy had always found that show to be dreadful; the police were always made out to be completely useless, barely able to catch even the most incompetent criminals. There was a documentary on Channel 4 about the starving children of Africa. Amy didn't want to watch that; it was much too depressing.

Despite knowing that nothing else would be on for at least another twenty minutes or so, Amy continued to click away on the remote control, flicking from one channel to the next, hoping that, by some small miracle, one of the programs may have changed to something actually worth watching.

That, of course, never happened.

"Do you want Coke or Vimto?" Tina called from the kitchen. She'd been gone for ages, Amy had almost forgotten she was there. This was Tina's house though, so it wasn't as if she would have actually left her there all alone.

"Is it Diet Coke?" Amy replied, raising her voice so that Tina might hear her from all the way down the hall. When Tina didn't reply,

Amy knew that she hadn't heard. She thought for a brief moment about shouting louder, then decided against it, deciding instead to take herself into the kitchen and see exactly what it was that Tina was doing that was taking her so long. She pushed herself up on the seat of the sofa behind her – she had found herself a not-so-comfortable spot on the floor, her back resting against the suite. Despite it not being all that comfortable, and despite having the far more luxurious sofa right there, once she'd sat herself down, she'd decided that she couldn't be bothered to move.

Back to her feet, Amy placed the remote onto the arm of the sofa, then headed out of the living room and along the hall. The floor of the kitchen was covered with a grey, tile effect linoleum, which she found to be cold on the bare soles of hr feet. Tina was bent over, leaning into the refrigerator, seemingly unaware of Amy's presence behind her. Amy approached slowly, so as not to give herself away. When she was within reach, she quickly darted forward and grabbed Tina by the waist. "Hey!" she said, as she dug her fingertips into Tina's flesh, just a little.

Tina practically jumped out of her skin. "Jesus Christ!" she said, the pitch of her voice jumping a few octaves. She spun on the spot, a terrified look on her face that made Amy feel bad for about half a nanosecond. "You scared the shit out of me!"

Amy laughed hard, her cheeks aching. She loved nothing more than tormenting Tina. "Sorry," she said, hardly able to contain herself. "I couldn't help myself. You make it too easy." Tina was still frowning, wholly unimpressed. She planted her hands firmly on her hips and tossed her hair to one side. She'd recently had it permed and had dyed it blonde, modelling her look after Madonna, or Cyndi Lauper. She pulled it off pretty well, in Amy's humble opinion. Still, the look of disdain currently etched on her face didn't suit her all too well.

"I asked if you wanted a drink," said Tina, puffing out her cheeks.

"I know. And I answered."

"You did? I didn't hear you."

"So I gathered, hence the reason I came in here to see what you were doing."

"Oh." Tina rolled her eyes and shook her head. She was wearing a pair of neon pink, plastic hoop earrings. She wore dark blue eyeshadow and a deep red lipstick. "Well," she said, "what *do* you want? Coke or Vimto?"

Amy laughed again. "I asked if it was Diet Coke."

"Oh, right." Tina turned and pulled the bottle out of the fridge, holding it up for Amy to see. The white label with red writing – as opposed to the usual red label with white writing – told Amy that this was, in fact, the new Diet variety. They said it was better for you than the regular Coca-Cola – less calories – although Amy wasn't entirely sure what that meant. Still, she thought it best to air on the side of caution and go with it; it was what all her friends were drinking after all.

Amy took the bottle from Tina and poured two glasses, one for each of them. She then returned it to Tina, who, in turn, returned it to the fridge. "You want crisps?" Tina asked.

"Sure," said Amy. "Why not?"

Tina dug through the cupboard by her knees and pulled out a multi-pack of Walkers Ready Salted. She pulled out one of the individual packs, tore it open and tipped it into a large, plastic bowl. She then repeated the process with three more packs, filling the bowl to the brim. With the two glasses of Diet Coke in hand, Amy headed back down the hall and into the lounge, followed closely by Tina, carrying the bowl of crisps.

"So," said Tina, as she dropped onto the sofa and immediately tucked her legs up beneath her. "What are we watching?" She picked up the remote and clicked the TV over to ITV, just in time to catch DCI Barnes reading some teenage drug dealer his rights – *'Anything you* do *say may be given in evidence…'*

"There's literally *nothing* on," sighed Amy, handing one of the glasses to Tina, before taking a seat on the sofa beside her.

"Yeah. There never is. I keep telling my parents they need to get cable, but they seem to think it'd be a waste of money."

Amy chuckled. "In all fairness, they're probably right!" Amy liked Tina's parents. Her mum was a nurse and her dad was a carpenter. They were both good people. They always treated her like a part of the family whenever she was around. They were out tonight, watching some show at the theatre.

"Well, just so long as they get MTV as soon as its available, I don't really care." Everybody had been raving about the music video to Michael Jackson's *Thriller*, but neither girl had yet to see it.

Amy sipped her Diet Coke as she watched Tina flipping through the channels, much like she had done herself, just a few short minutes ago. It was as if Tina didn't really believe her. There had to be *something* on, right?

No, there didn't.

"Oh, shit!" said Tina, a sudden sense of excitement radiating from her. She was staring at Amy with her eyebrows raised almost beyond her hairline. Amy found this somewhat unnerving; Tina looked half deranged.

"What is it?" asked Amy, not sure if she really wanted to know the answer.

"I know *exactly* what we can watch!" Tina jumped up from the sofa, nearly spilling her drink and causing a number of crisps to jump from the bowl and scatter across the floor. She placed her glass onto the oak sideboard, then dropped to her knees before the TV.

Amy leant forward and picked up the crisps that Tina had dropped. Her mum wouldn't be best pleased, having to come home and find discarded food stomped into her carpet. Having gathered them up, Amy placed them delicately onto the arm of the sofa, where she would remember to pick them up and dispose of them later. "What are you going on about?" she asked Tina, rubbing her hands together, an effort to remove the excess salt from her palms.

Tina had pulled open the cupboard doors of the TV unit and was rooting around inside, clearly on a mission to find something. "You'll never guess what Mikey brought home the other night."

Moreso now, Amy wasn't sure she wanted to know. Mikey was Tina's older brother. She had always found him quite attractive. At twenty-one though, he was four years older than she was, and, in her own mind, way out of her league. But he was into some weird stuff, and thinking to herself at that very moment, she had no idea what it was that Tina might be about to retrieve from that cupboard.

"Ah!" said Tina, seemingly out of breath from the effort she'd put into hunting through the cupboard. "Found it!" She sat back onto her heels, then stood. In her hand was a flimsy Tesco carrier bag. She reached into the bag, removed the contents, then tossed the bag itself aside.

Amy looked at what Tina was now holding in her hand. It took her a moment to recognise the black slabs of plastic, but then she realised that they were video cassette tapes. "Oh, God," she said, dreading the worst. "Please tell me that isn't porno. The *last* thing I want is to sit here watching porno films with you. No offence."

Tina scoffed a laugh. "None taken. No, of course it's not porno. They're video nasties."

Amy raised her eyebrows. She could feel the frown furrowing her forehead. "Seriously?" she said. She wasn't sure which was worse; perhaps it would've been better if they *were* porno films.

"Yeah! You wanna watch one?"

"Aren't they saying those films are dangerous?"

"What they're saying is that they *could* turn the people who watch them into psychopathic murderers. Somehow, I doubt that."

The video nasties had been talked about a lot in the press over the previous year or so. Most of them were violent horror films. Many featured sex and violence and murder and rape and torture. With no story or decent acting to carry them along, they all relied on blood and guts and naked girls to pull in an audience. Some people felt they could pose a threat to society. As drastic as that sounded, unlike Tina, Amy wasn't entirely sure that it was completely beyond the realms of possibility. As such, and to the best of her knowledge, she'd never watched any of them. Most of her friends – Tina included – had seen some of them though; some days, it was all they talked about during their lunch break in the college cafeteria. She really didn't understand why they would *want* to discuss how *this* character was decapitated with a rusty length of barbed wire, or how *that* character was eviscerated by a masked lunatic armed with a scythe, all while eating their lunch; it was enough to turn her stomach. “Really?” she said, a sense of trepidation building in the pit of her stomach. “Do we have to?”

“Why not? You’re not *really* scared, are you?”

The truth was, Amy *was* a little scared. Why would all those people be saying how bad they were if it wasn’t true? But then, perhaps that was just a little bit paranoid. She knew lots of people who had watched them – or claimed to have watched them, at least – and none of them had gone crazy. It didn’t seem likely that a shitty horror film could have such an effect on an otherwise sane individual.

But perhaps it wasn’t worth the risk.

“I’m not scared,” snorted Amy, as if the mere suggestion was beyond ridiculous. “I just don’t get why people would want to watch other people being murdered, that’s all.”

“Nobody *really* gets murdered. They’re actors, you know?”

“*You don’t say*,” Amy oozed with sarcasm. “Where did Mikey get them from anyway. I thought it was illegal to rent them out now.”

Tina nodded. “It is. But when did that ever stop anybody?”

Amy frowned.

“Come on,” groaned Tina. “It’s fun to be scared sometimes!”

“But they’re not scary. They’re just disgusting.”

“How would *you* know, if *you’ve* never watched them?” Clearly she was confident in the knowledge that there was no good answer to that one.

And Amy knew it too. “I *do* read the newspapers,” she said, despite knowing that didn’t really count for much. “They say…”

“What *they* say,” Tina interrupted, “is a load of old bollocks. How about you watch one and decide for yourself?”

Tina stood there with her eyebrows raised, and her hands on her hips, as if to say *‘I’m right, and you know I am.’* Amy had to admit, Tina *was* right. She hadn’t watched any of these movies, so she had no idea what they were really like. The newspapers were renowned for their lies and their bullshit; it stood to reason that their opinions on video nasties were just as much drivel as their take on the miner's strike that had been dragging on for the past six months.

Amy sighed, defeated. "Alright. Fine. What have you got?"

Tina hopped up and down and clapped her hands together, clearly excited at the prospect of showing Amy her very first video nasty. "Alright, let's see." Each of the tapes was housed in a generic black plastic case. A simple card sleeve slid into the front of the case displayed the name and logo of the local video shop; a yellow moon and stars on a dark blue background, the words 'Video Magic' stencilled below. Tina read the title from the spine of the first tape. "*Evilspeak*" she said.

"Never heard of it. Is it any good?"

"No idea. I've never heard of it either." She slid the next tape from the bottom of the pile and shifted it to the top. Again, she read the spine. "*The Beyond*. I think it's about zombies."

"Zombies? Sounds *amazing*," said Amy, rolling her eyes sarcastically.

Tina read the spine of the final tape. "*The House On The Edge Of The Park*."

"Oh, I think I've heard of that one. Is that the one with the girls who get raped and murdered, and then their parents take revenge on the killers?"

"Erm… No," said Tina, a look of confusion on her face that Amy found to be almost hilarious. "That's *The Last House On The Left*."

"Yeah, *The Last House On The Left*. That's the one I was thinking of."

"Well, they're pretty similar, I guess. In fact, they both star the same actor in the role of the main villain. But, I mean, how is it that you've even heard of either of them?"

Amy had read about *The Last House On The Left* in one of those newspaper articles. It was one of the most cited examples of just how 'nasty' the video nasties could be, along with *Cannibal Holocaust* and *The Evil Dead*. "Maybe I know more about video nasties than you think I do," she said.

"Alright. So, which one should we watch?"

Amy didn't particularly want to watch any of them. *The Bill* would be finished soon; maybe something worth watching might come on afterwards. But she couldn't tell Tina that; she'd never let her live it down. "Well, I'm not really in the mood for rape and murder right now, and I've never heard of the *Evil… Evil…*"

"*Evilspeak*," said Tina, completing the title that Amy had already forgotten.

"*Evilspeak*. So, maybe we should go with the zombies?"

"*The Beyond*?" said Tina, nodding her head, suitably impressed. "You got it." She placed the videos onto the top of the TV cabinet, and removed the cassette of *The Beyond* from its case. She then placed the cassette into the deck of the VCR and pushed it down into the belly of the machine. She pressed play and the VCR roared to life, the tape whirring from somewhere deep inside.

A fuzzy, static-filled image appeared on the screen of the TV. Lines buzzed from top to bottom. It took a few moments for the tracking of the VCR to automatically adjust itself, revealing the picture beneath the snowy blanket. The logo of the distribution company flickered on-screen; '*Vampix - A Videomedia Company*'. A trailer then began. There was a weird looking boy in a strange house. A decapitated head. A blood-soaked man, stabbed with scissors. Was that a zombie? Whatever it was, Amy thought it looked entirely ridiculous. The title of the film flashed up several times during the trailer; it was called *The House By The Cemetery*. "Another house?" said Amy, smirking. "Why do they all have the word '*house*' in the title?"

"Because houses are spooky," laughed Tina. She scooped a handful of crisps from the bowl, stuffed them into her mouth, then washed them down with a sip of her Diet Coke. She then offered the crisps to Amy, who took some for herself.

On the TV, the film started. A group of men rowed across a river. A man worked on his painting; a picture of some desolate wasteland. The men in the boat had torches and pitchforks, reminding Amy of a witch hunt. Those men then stormed into the hotel in which the artist was working. They dragged the artist down into the basement and nailed him to the wall. Blood poured from the wounds in his wrists. It was quite a grizzly effect, one which Amy found to be quite unsettling. The men then covered the artist in some corrosive substance, perhaps quicklime, melting the skin from his face. This effect was less impressive. It was clear that the actor had been swapped out for what looked like some miscellaneous shop mannequin, splattered with red paint.

Amy sipped her drink. Tina crunched her way through the crisps.

On the screen, a man took a fall from a scaffold, having seen a woman with white eyes staring at him through a window. In Tina's kitchen, the phone rang. Tina jumped first, nearly spilling the crisps once again. The sudden, involuntary movement of her body caused Amy to jump too. This time, Amy did spill her drink. "Shit!" she said, hopping up from the sofa, the cool wetness of the cola soaking in through her leggings.

"Oops. Sorry about that," said Tina, grinning from ear to ear. It was quite apparent that she wasn't sorry at all. She crossed over to the VCR and hit the pause button. In the kitchen, the phone rang once again. "Come on. Let's get you a towel."

Tina led Amy down the hallway once again, and back into the kitchen. The phone was still ringing. Tina grabbed the red-and-white tea towel from the worktop beside the sink and tossed it to Amy. Amy caught it and began to pat the wet patch in her lap. Tina answered the phone halfway through the next ring. It was mounted on the wall beside the door. She lifted the receiver and held it to her ear. "Hello?" she said. She looked to Amy, her eyebrows raised. "Hello*ooooooo*?"

Amy frowned as she continued to dry herself off. "Who is it?"

Tina shrugged her shoulders. "Who is this? I can hear you, you know? You sound like you have asthma. You might wanna get that checked out."

"Just hang up."

"See ya later, creep," Tina said, before returning the receiver to its cradle.

"There was nobody there?" asked Amy, already fully aware of what the answer would be.

Tina shook her head. "Nope. I mean, there *was* somebody there. I could hear them breathing. I guess they just didn't want to talk to me."

"That's weird."

"Maybe they were just too enthralled by my sensual voice," Tina giggled. She took the towel from Amy. "Are you dry?"

"As best as I think I can be."

"Cool. Come on. Let's get back to the film."

Amy wasn't sure how much time had passed before the phone rang again. The woman in the film – her name was Liza; she'd inherited the hotel in which all these bizarre goings on had occurred – had just found a rotting corpse nailed to the wall of Room 36. Tina didn't jump when the phone rang this time. Instead, she groaned. "Jesus. This best not be that heavy-breathing freak again."

"If it is, maybe you could invite him 'round," laughed Amy. "I imagine he'd be the sort of person to enjoy this film."

"You're not enjoying it?"

"Me? Of course! How could I *not* enjoy it? It's a masterpiece. Possibly the greatest film ever made."

"Was that sarcasm by any chance?"

"How did you guess?"

The phone continued to ring. Tina headed out of the living room.

"You want me to pause this?" Amy called after her as she left the room.

"Nah. It's fine. I'm sure I'll catch up."

Amy watched the film, but paid it little attention; she was more interested in listening to Tina answer the phone in the other room. "Hello?" she said, just as she had last time. And then, once again, followed that up with, "Hello*oooooo*?" Nobody there again. Amy found this slightly worrying. Why would somebody be calling and then refusing to talk? What was the point? Most likely it was one of their friends, just trying to play some sort of prank. Still, it was a strange thing for somebody to do.

"Is this gonna go on all night," Tina asked the unresponsive caller. "Because I'm getting bored already. Okay. I'm hanging up now. Bye."

Amy heard the click of the receiver hooking back onto the cradle. And then… nothing.

On the TV, a man was having his face chewed off by a swarm of plastic spiders. Amy leaned out over the side of the sofa and looked down the hall towards the kitchen. "Tina?" she called. "Are you okay?"

No response.

Amy stood. She could feel a sense of concern growing inside her. "Tina?" Why wasn't she responding? Nothing bad could've happened to her in the past thirty seconds. Surely not. Slowly, Amy began to creep along the hall. She was listening closely, hoping she might just hear Tina clattering around in one of the cupboards, perhaps looking for some more crisps. As she thought about it, Tina hadn't heard her calling a little while ago; this was probably just the same thing. "Tina?" she said, as she stepped into the kitchen.

"BOO!"

Amy screamed as Tina jumped out from behind the doorframe, her hands raised above her head, her fingers twisted into monstrous claws. But then she was laughing hysterically. "Gotcha," she said, hardly able to breathe.

"That's not even funny!" said Amy, her voice almost a whimper.

"Yes it was," smirked Tina. "And now you know how it feels."

Amy supposed she deserved it. She rolled her eyes, a gesture meant just as much for herself as it was for Tina. "I'm guessing that was *lover-boy* on the phone again."

"Yep. You know me – I love the strong, silent type."

Amy laughed, although she wasn't entirely sure the situation was at all funny. If anything, whoever it was that kept calling could really do with locking up. "You coming to watch the film, or what? I'm assuming these zombies are going to show up soon."

"Yeah," said Tina. "I just gotta pop to the little girls' room. You carry on. I'll just be a minute." And with that, she passed by the living room and headed up the stairs.

Amy went and sat back down in the living room. The picture on the TV was buzzing with static. When it cleared, a woman was lying on the floor of a morgue, a jar of acid spilled on the table above, the contents leaking over the edge and turning her face to a bloody mush. It was quite gross.

This stupid film didn't make any sense. It wasn't even scary.

A loud thud shook the ceiling, causing Amy's heartrate to double. She looked up, as dust filtered down through the air, loosened from the artex.

Slowly, Amy stood. For some reason unbeknownst to her, a sense of apprehension was seemingly rooting her to the spot. "Tina?" she called. "You okay?"

There was no response.

Her anxiety building, Amy crept along the hall to the bottom of the stairs. There, she once again called up, and once again received no reply. It occurred to her that Tina was most likely trying to play another prank on her. If she was, then it wasn't very funny. "If this is some kind of trick," said Amy, as she cautiously made her way up the stairs. "Then I'm going to kill you! Seriously, if you jump out at me again, you're dead."

Tina still didn't respond.

Along the landing, the door to the bathroom stood ajar, the harsh, white light from inside the room spilling out into the darkened hallway.

Slowly, Amy pushed the door open. "Tina?"

The bathroom was empty.

There was another noise from somewhere further along the landing, the sound of shuffling coming from Tina's room. Amy could feel her heart hammering against her ribcage. Something was telling her that this just wasn't right, that she ought to get out of there, just run away.

No – that was stupid. It was just Tina messing around.

"Tina? What the hell are you playing at? Come out now, you're just being dumb."

Amy made her way across the landing and pushed open the door to Tina's bedroom.

This was a room that Amy had been in a million times before. Numerous posters adorned the walls – *Duran Duran* and *Culture Club* and *Wham!* and *Frankie Goes To Hollywood.* A black-and-white TV set sat on the dressing table, a series of neon lights surrounding the mirror. A noticeboard hung on the wall above the bed, dozens of photographs held in place with drawing pins, each one showing Tina and her friends. Amy herself was in many of them.

And there, on the bed, laid Tina's corpse.

Her torso was awash with blood, the cotton of the top she'd been wearing completely saturated, adhering to the skin of her belly and breasts. A pair of scissors protruded from her chest, wedged in between her ribs. The skin beneath her top was ragged, multiple lacerations having shredded the flesh like cabbage. The blood had splattered onto her pale, lifeless face, streaking along her cheek. Her eyes were still open, staring into some unfathomable void, entirely dead.

Amy screamed.

Only then did she see Tina's killer, watching her from the corner of the room, the shape of a man, dressed entirely in black.

She had no time to process what she was seeing. She turned and ran.

But the killer was right behind her. She could hear him, his feet pounding the floor just a few inches away. He was grunting, short of breath, driving himself after her.

Amy swung around the corner of stairs with such velocity that she almost lost her footing. If it weren't for her grasp on the banister, then she almost certainly would have gone flying, no doubt breaking her neck on impact. As it was, she maintained her balance and scooted down the stairs, taking them two at a time.

The killer followed, growing ever nearer.

The front door was right there. Amy ran for it, wrenching the handle downward, only to find that it was locked.

Shit!

The killer was right behind her now, waiting at the bottom of the stairs, stalking slowly towards her. It was a man; Amy was sure of it. The broad shoulders gave him away. But Amy couldn't see his face – he was wearing a black balaclava, the itchy wool of the material covering the entirety of his head, leaving only his eyes and mouth visible. He wore a black jacket and black trousers and black gloves, not an inch of skin on show.

In his right hand he held a straight razor, light glistening as it reflected from the blade.

Terror ripped through Amy's body, tearing her heart in two. Tears streamed down her cheeks now, her every breath racked and painful in her lungs.

But she couldn't give up. She had to try to escape.

She ran for the kitchen. The back door was here, her only other means of escape, save for her trying to scramble out of a window. Amy slammed into the back door, pulling at the handle, once again finding it to be locked. But the key was there, protruding from the lock, just beneath the handle. She turned it. The latch clicked into place and the door swung open.

Amy crossed the threshold into the garden, escaping into the cool air of the night.

Except…

The killer's fingers wove their way into her hair, yanking her backwards, back into the kitchen. Her muscles weak, Amy could do little as her body drove involuntarily sideways, her feet struggling for purchase on the linoleum. Her body flung forward, crashing painfully into the sink, her ribs cracking as they collided with the corner of the countertop. Then the killer had her again. He pulled her to her feet, then slammed her down, face first into the drying rack, where numerous plates and glasses and cutlery had been placed. A surge of agony pulsed through Amy's body as she tumbled awkwardly to the floor, dragging much of the broken kitchen utensils down on top of her.

She could taste blood on her tongue. A series of lacerations littered her palms and zig-zagged up her forearms. A nasty cut had opened up on her cheek, where her face had raked across an upturned breadknife.

Dazed, she looked up at the killer, standing over her now, his razorblade brandished, ready to kill. "Please…" she muttered. "No…"

But then something caught his eye. Pausing momentarily, he stepped over Amy's prone body.

Knowing that this might be her only chance to escape, Amy moved as quickly as her battered body would allow. She rolled to her front and scrambled to her knees, crawling towards the back door.

She knew she shouldn't have looked back, shouldn't have wasted those precious seconds in doing so, but curiosity go the better of her. She looked back to see the killer rooting through Tina's dad's toolbox. What he retrieved from inside sent a shiver down her spine.

An electric drill.

The killer plugged the drill into the wall socket and pulled the trigger. The motor whirred as blue sparks flickered from the back of the aluminium body.

A sickness rising in her stomach, the fear of her impending death spurring her on, Amy crawled quicker now, dragging her beaten body towards the door, pain coursing through her veins, emanating from the wounds that littered her arms and hands.

The killer stalked slowly towards her, his finger never straying from the trigger, the obstreperous racket pounding her eardrums ceaselessly. He was on top of her then, grabbing at her shoulder, flipping her onto her back. There was nothing Amy could do to stop him. He placed his free hand on the side of her face and dropped to one knee, his full weight pinning her down.

Amy gritted her teeth as the savage point of the whirring drill bit neared. It was less than an inch from her when the plug pulled loose from the socket, the electrical flex having reached the extent of its length. With the power cut from the drill, the bit stopped spinning.

The killer grunted his annoyance as he stood, marching over to the where the drill had been plugged into the wall.

Amy rolled over once more, tried to scramble for the door. But the killer grabbed her by the ankle and dragged her back into the middle of the kitchen, her body lubricated by the copious blood she had spilled.

Then he was on her once again.

"No," moaned Amy, gagging on her own phlegm. "P-please don't do this. Please… D-don't *kill* me…"

The killer ignored her.

He pulled the trigger of the drill.

He grabbed a handful of her hair and yanked, pulling her head back. He reached around and pressed the point of the drill into her forehead. The drill bit chewed easily through Amy's skin, tearing it like paper, peeling it away from the bone beneath.

A cacophony of gruesome noises filled Amy's ears – the squelching of flesh, the cracking of bone.

Amy screamed, an excruciating pain shredding her nerves. The warmth of blood poured over her face. The drill bit ground into her skull then, splintering the bone. To Amy, it felt as if her head was expanding, an immense pressure building around her brain, forcing the bone outward. She could hear her cranium cracking, even over the cacophonous noise of the drill.

She opened her eyes one last time, and looked into the eyes of the killer. They were black. There was nothing there; no recognition, no life, no humanity.

The steel of the drill bit ripped through Amy's brain, mulching the soft grey matter, and finally bringing an end to her torturous suffering.

In the lounge, on the TV, Catriona McColl and David Warbeck ran through the halls of a hospital, surrounded by hordes of the living dead.

--- --- --- --- --- --- --- --- --- --- --- ---

We have to consider all the facts. Do we really want our children watching these movies? Do we even have any idea as to what psychological damage might be done to their underdeveloped minds? These films give children a warped understanding of the difference between right and wrong. If they can watch a man drill into somebody's brain in a film like Driller Killer, *or they can watch as a teenage girl is brutally raped in* Last House On The Left, *then what's stopping them from doing these same things themselves? This is about safety. It is about our safety, and the safety of our children. We need to keep these films out of the hands of children. Who knows what might happen if we don't?*

Margret Whitehead, conservative activist and author of 'Violence On Video: The End Of Morality?'

CHAPTER TWO:

UNHINGED

Helen stood before the enormous pane of glass that was the front window of the Tandy Electrical store on Oakhill High Street, one of a series of stores that lined both sides of the road. Beyond the window, a dozen television sets had been arranged in such a way that any passers-by – and, ergo, any potential customers – could see them. They were staggered left to right, and had been positioned at two different heights, the back row seated on some kind of raised platform. Each TV was tuned to the same channel, each playing the same footage, each one perfectly synchronised with the next.

A talk show played on the screens. The host of the show – a wiry-looking man, with slick hair and wire-frame glasses – walked amongst the audience, which appeared to consist of a wide variety of people, all different ages and races. Helen herself was seventeen – some of the people in this audience couldn't have been much older than her, nineteen or twenty perhaps. The host moved from one person to the next, holding his microphone out towards them, so that they could ask a question of the four men seated on the stage before them.

Of the four men on the stage, three of them were significantly older than the other. The odd-one-out couldn't have been any older than twenty-five. He wore a *Metallica* t-shirt and his hair hung past his ears in thick, scraggy waves.

The title of the segment was displayed at the bottom of the screen: 'VIDEO NASTIES: ARE THEY EVIL?'

The host held his microphone out to one of the younger members of the audience, a guy with long black hair and an acne-riddled face. "So," scoffed the kid on the TV, "if what you're saying *is* true, and these movies really *are* gonna turn us all into a bunch of raving psychos, then why haven't they had any effect on you?"

The other members of the audience – the younger members, specifically – all nodded their heads in unison, muttering their agreement.

On the stage, a rotund man with a balding head and a thick moustache sat forward in his seat, adjusting his glasses, pushing them back up along the bridge of his nose. He had been introduced at the start of the segment as Gary Smart, a conservative Member of Parliament. "These movies haven't had any effect on *me*," he smirked, as if the answer should have been obvious, "because *I* haven't watched any of them!"

The youngest member of the panel burst out into a fit of laughter, shaking his head as if this were the most ridiculous thing he'd ever heard. "What do you mean – *'you haven't watched them'*?" he snorted, incredulously. "How can you *possibly* have any kind of opinion on the matter, if you don't even know what's in these films?" This guy had been introduced as Adam Chambers, independent filmmaker.

"I don't *need* to have seen them, to know what's in them," retorted the MP. "No respectable adult, with anything more than half a brain cell, would ever lower themselves to watch such utter depravity."

At this remark, most of the audience began booing. Helen noticed that it was mainly the older members of the audience who seemed to remain quiet. They seemed to have stern looks on their faces, like they were fully in agreement with the MP. She herself didn't really hold any opinion on the matter. She knew of the 'video nasties' – those violent horror films that politicians across the country were trying so hard to get banned – but she hadn't ever watched any of them. She'd seen bits and pieces, of course; she'd watched the opening scene of *The Burning*, and she'd seen various clips from *Cannibal Holocaust*. She'd even gotten part way through *The Evil Dead*, but she'd had to bow out after a girl got raped by a tree.

It was cold outside. Helen was wearing a scarf, but still the chill seemed to be getting to her. She shoved her hands into her coat pockets as a shiver ran down her spine, a cool autumnal breeze rolling along the high street.

On the TV screens, another audience member – a girl this time, her jet-black hair cut into a short bob, dark mascara lining her eyes – had the microphone before them. "But," she said, "if *you* haven't seen these films, then who is it that's telling you about what happens in them? And, more to the point, why haven't *they* gone crazy?"

Another of the older men on the stage raised his liver-spotted hand, indicating that he wished to answer. He looked frail. His head was completely bald on top, with wispy grey hairs around the back and sides. Wire frame glasses perched precariously on the tip of his razor-sharp nose. He had been introduced as William Mitchell, professor of psychology. "There is a very simple explanation for this," he said, lowering his hand and lacing his fingers, laying them across his lap. "We believe that adult minds are much better suited to processing this sort of violent imagery than adolescent minds. They are more developed. More refined."

Once again, the youngest member of the panel – Adam – shook his head. He leaned forward from his seat, looking along the stage to his much-elder counterpart. "So when does that happen?" he said, his eyebrows raised.

"When does what happen?"

"When does an adolescent mind become more 'refined'? At what age? Eighteen? Is an eighteen-year-old an adult? Do *they* have an adult mind?"

The elderly man shrugged his shoulders. "It's not quite so clear cut as that. Although the law states that, yes, an eighteen-year-old is an adult, their brains may not develop until much later in life."

"But adults *can* watch these films, without being transformed into deranged maniacs, right?"

"Yes. Of course."

The young guy shook his head once again, as if he were trying to get all the pieces of this puzzle to fit. "So then why shouldn't *they* be allowed to? An outright ban on these moves would prevent everybody from watching them, even those adults who - according to the '*science*' - are perfectly able to enjoy them, without being turned into some kind of lunatic."

The audience clapped.

The younger members, anyway.

"Do we, as a civilised society, really *want* people to enjoy this sort of filth?" asked the other older gentleman on the stage.

"This isn't about preventing adults from seeing these movies," interjected Gary Smart. "But without regulation, it is impossible for us to stop children from seeing them, too."

"So we should just ban them outright, so that nobody can view them?" said Adam.

"Exactly! As responsible adults, we should be willing to accept some restrictions on our lives, in order to protect our children."

"But I don't have any children! Why should it be *my* responsibility to protect *your* kids?"

"I don't think you understand –it's not just children. We have sufficient evidence to suggest that this kind of depraved imagery can cause the mental breakdown of animals, too. Our pets could be at risk! There are even studies that show these movies may have a negative impact on house plants!"

Adam looked around the studio, looking as if he thought he himself may have lost his mind. "Have you heard yourself?" he said. "I don't think I've ever heard anything so ridiculous in all my life! I thought you people were supposed to be intelligent. How is it even possible for you to be *this* stupid?"

An argument broke out then, the four members of the panel all shouting over each other, the audience members bellowing their own opinions. The host ran around the studio, waving his arms, trying to calm the situation. It was utter chaos.

A hand landed on Helen's shoulder, startling her.

"Sorry," said Lorraine, the smile on her face betraying the insincerity of her apology. "I didn't mean to scare you. You okay?"

"Yeah," said Anna. "You seemed a little 'zoned out' for a minute there."

Helen shook her head. "I'm fine. I was just watching the TV."

Lorraine scoffed. "Ugghh… Those things will rot your brain."

"What?" laughed Helen. "Since *when*? You don't watch TV anymore?"

"Not out in the middle of the street I don't."

Helen, Lorraine and Anna had been inseparable for years. They had known each other since middle school, where the three of them had become best friends. They had been there for each other as they had each gotten their first kiss – naturally, Helen had been the last. They had been there for each other as they had each gotten their first period – again, Helen had been the last. They had been there for each other as they had each lost their virginity – this time, Helen hadn't been last. She had, in fact, been the first to have sex. She'd been fifteen when it had happened. Bret – her boyfriend at the time – had been quite insistent that they ought to make love, to ensure that their bond would never be broken. That was total bullshit of course; two weeks after they'd first slept together, Bret had dumped her and moved onto somebody else.

Lorraine and Anna had been there for Helen then, too. They'd comforted her, they'd been her shoulder to cry on. They'd made fun of Bret and the tiny micro-penis that Lorraine was sure he had hidden away in his pants. They'd laughed so much that Helen had almost forgotten the hurt she'd felt when Bret had broken the bond that he himself had insisted they shared.

Of course, after the deed was initially done, Lorraine and Anna had wanted all the gory details. But, as Helen had told them then, there *weren't* any gory details to share. It was fine. It was nice. It hurt, and – yes – she had bled a bucketful. She didn't believe she had climaxed. It hadn't lasted long; no more than three minutes. Helen didn't think that would be enough time for her to orgasm. Bret had at least had the decency to wear a condom. As such, Helen couldn't answer when

Lorraine had asked what it felt like to have sperm swimming up your vagina.

So, yes – they were best friends. They knew every intimate detail about each other's lives (Lorraine's first sexual encounter had supposedly been amazing, while Anna's had been downright awful).

Lorraine was the most popular of the three girls. At least, that were true when it came to the boys. She had long blonde hair, which she almost always crimped, and tied back with a scrunchie. She was always impeccably dressed; today she wore a black vest top, a denim jacket, and a short denim skirt, with bright pink tights underneath, to keep the cold off her long, slender legs. Her breasts were full and perky, to the point that she hardly ever wore a bra. Of course, it was this that the boys liked most about her.

Sometimes, Helen found herself jealous of the attention that Lorraine received. Other times, she was glad to not be on the receiving end.

Anna wore a pair of baggy, high-waisted jeans, a thick leather belt nipping them in over her hips. She wore a light grey woollen jumper, which mostly hid her figure. She wasn't as confident as Lorraine, or Helen for that matter. She'd never had a real boyfriend. As far as Helen was aware, that boy that Anna had lost her virginity to had been the only boy she'd ever been with. Moreso, as best she knew, that was the one and only time Anna had had sex.

Helen wasn't quiet as reserved as Anna, but she most certainly wasn't as 'out there' as Lorraine. She wore nice clothes that showed off her figure just the right amount. Never too slutty, but enough to make the boys take a second glance on occasion. She had shoulder-length brunette hair, which she had, today, decided to wear in a side-ponytail.

Lorrain scoffed as she watched what was playing on the TVs behind the shop window. "Ugghh," she moaned. "Why do people watch this shit?"

"Video Nasties?" asked Helen, unsure of what she actually meant.

"No. This fucking chat show. It's just a group of morons, arguing with a bunch of idiots, about some shit that nobody even cares about." She shook her head, almost in disgust.

Helen laughed. "Ohh-kayy… So, anyway – did you get what you wanted?"

Lorraine and Anna had been into the corner shop at the end of the street, to buy cigarettes. Anna reached into her pocket and pulled out a packet of B&H Special Filters. "You want one?"

"Sure," said Helen, her eyes flicking back and forth along the street. "Not here though – my mum will kill me if she finds out I've been smoking." Helen's mum was ultra-over-protective. She wouldn't like her smoking, not one bit. She wanted to keep her wrapped up in a protective bubble. If she had it her way, Helen probably wouldn't ever leave the house.

Still, this was somewhat understandable. The trauma of what had happened to her all those years ago on Halloween night still resonated deep inside.

Today was October 27th – Halloween was just a few days away. Helen's mother's over-protectivity would only increase exponentially over the coming days.

With her mother being so over-bearing, Helen couldn't risk being seen. She knew she was just being paranoid, but she always had a feeling that somebody might be watching her. If that somebody should go and tell her mother that she'd been smoking, then all hell was likely to break loose.

So, the three girls headed away from the high street, and into the park, cutting across the fields towards the college. Once they were clearly out of sight, Anna distributed the cigarettes between them, then offered a lighter. Helen took it, rolling the flint until the flame popped. She lit her cigarette and inhaled deeply. She didn't exactly like the taste of tobacco, but the nicotine did feel good as it started to course through her veins.

She handed the lighter to Lorraine, who promptly lit her own cigarette, before returning the lighter to Anna.

The walk through the park was pleasant. Very few of the trees still retained their leaves. Of those that did, even fewer were still green. Most of the leaves were orange and brown, a thick layer of them coating the footpath like a blanket. The footpath encircled the perimeter of the pond, ducks and geese floating serenely on the surface, waiting for anybody who might offer them chunks of bread. The girls stuck to the outermost pathway, away from the scores of people passing through the park. This way, Helen felt more confident that nobody who knew her mother might see her smoking.

They'd finished their cigarettes by the time they reached the other side of the park, each of them having dropped the smouldering remains, extinguishing them underfoot. Beyond the park, another road ran behind a cluster of small shops and takeaway restaurants, before arriving at the college.

As they passed through the carpark, Helen noticed an ITN news van parked up towards the entrance. The rear doors were open and two men were busy organising equipment, one of them loading tape into a camera. A woman that Helen vaguely recognised was crouched down beside the passenger side door, applying her lipstick in the wing mirror.

"What's that all about?" said Anna, as if she had read the thought directly from Helen's mind.

"No idea," said Helen. "Did something happen here?"

Lorraine shrugged her shoulders nonchalantly.

The entrance to the college had been draped in orange and black streamers, with a sign above the door that read 'HAPPY HALLOWEEN!'. Carboard cut-outs of pumpkins and ghosts had been stuck in the windows, facing outward.

Chris and Ryan were waiting just inside. As soon as they saw the girls entering, they rushed over. "Oh my God! Did you hear?" said Chris, before hooking his arm around Lorraine's waist and planting a kiss on her lips. He was her current boyfriend. They'd been together for a few months now, which, as best Helen could recall, was probably the longest relationship Lorraine had ever had. Chris was a handsome guy. His hair was neat, brushed to one side, cascading down over his ears. He wore a rugby shirt, striped in blue and white, which clung to his muscular frame.

"Hear what?" asked Helen, genuinely puzzled, but certain that this had something to do with the news van parked outside.

"Amy Stone and Tina Wilkinson were murdered last night."

Helen's first thought was that Chris must be joking, but the look on his face was entirely sincere. "Oh my God. Seriously?"

Chris nodded.

"Tina's parents found them at home," said Ryan. "It was a blood bath. Apparently, they'd been chopped into pieces."

A sick smile crossed Ryan's face. He was a nice enough guy, but he'd always been a bit of an oddball. He was wearing tight, stonewashed jeans, and a t-shirt adorned with an image of Michelangelo from the 'Teenage Mutant Hero Turtles', slurping the cheese from a slice of pizza, the word 'COWABUNGA!' written beneath in an explosion of colour. Ryan wore this shirt entirely unironically, what with him being a huge fan of those heroes in a half-shell, despite falling well outside of the target demographic.

"Do they know who did it?" asked Lorraine.

"No idea," said Chris. "They think it was just some lunatic who broke into the house. Probably a burglary gone wrong."

"That sucks…" Lorraine scoffed, shaking her head.

"Well," said Anna. "I hope they catch whoever did it. I don't want to be walking the streets while there's a maniac on the loose."

"Don't worry Anna," laughed Ryan. "It sounds to me like this killer only goes for the pretty girls."

"Gee, thanks," snorted Anna, nudging Ryan with her elbow.

Helen could feel herself frowning, a sense of apprehension growing within her. She didn't like the way they were joking around, when two of their friends – admittedly, Amy and Tina weren't in their immediate circle of friends – had been brutally murdered. "Come on, guys," she said, her voice wavering. "That could've been any of us.

You wouldn't like it if people were laughing and joking after finding out you'd been murdered."

"I don't think I'd really care," said Ryan, entirely straight-faced. "You know, since I'd be dead."

"Well, let's hope they come for you next," chuckled Chris.

"*Fuuuuccck* you."

A bell rang out through the corridor, indicating that it was time for them to get to class. Chris kissed Lorraine once more, before parting ways. Lorraine, Anna and Ryan then headed off along one corridor, while Chris and Helen went in the opposite direction, themselves splitting off once they reached the next hall.

Helen spent most of the day distracted from her classes, her mind more focused on those two dead girls, and their poor, devastated parents.

And then she thought of her own mother. Best not to tell her.

She'd only worry.

--- --- --- --- --- --- --- --- --- --- --- ---

As adults we should be allowed the freedom to make our own choices. Of course, nobody is advocating for kids to be allowed to watch the so-called Video Nasties. *But, let's be honest – do we really believe that these movies can have such a negative impact on a child's mental welfare? And if we do, where's the proof? Kids have already been watching these films, and, so far as I'm aware, we haven't yet had a spate of mass murders committed by these children, have we? Why not lock some kids in a room and let them watch* I Spit On Your Grave*? Then we'll see what might really happen.*

David Copley, entertainment journalist

and writer for 'Video News Weekly'

CHAPTER THREE:

BLOOD BATH

It didn't take long for news to spread through the small town of Oakhill, especially when the news was of such a gruesome nature.

Wendy had heard it from Sally, her neighbour from three doors down. Sally had apparently heard it from Judy, a friend of hers, whom she had bumped into down at the local Safeway. God only knew where Judy had heard it from. Not that any of it really mattered; Wendy knew the parents of one of those girls, so she'd been able to confirm it for herself.

Wendy's daughter, Helen, had played netball with one of the murdered girls back in middle school. She and Amy had been quite close at one point, Amy having come over for dinner on a handful of occasions. Wendy could still picture that cute little girl, dressed in her dungarees, her hair tied in plaits, sitting at their breakfast table, slurping on the strawberry milkshake she always made whenever her daughter had friends over. But their friendship hadn't blossomed quite as Wendy might've liked. Nowadays, Helen hardly ever talked about Amy – not that she ever really talked about *any* of her friends.

Despite this, Wendy had remained in touch with Sandra – Amy's mother. They were both members of the same book club, so they saw each other at least once a week. Wendy had called Sandra the very moment she'd heard the news. Sandra hadn't answered the phone herself; it was a woman who identified herself as Sandra's sister-in-law. Sandra was unavailable, but the woman Wendy had spoken with had confirmed that – yes – Sandra's precious baby girl had indeed been murdered.

Wendy felt sick to her stomach. An uncomfortable feeling writhed in her gut. She couldn't imagine just how devastated that poor girl's parents must be. She could think of nothing worse. For a moment, she imagined what it might be like if her own daughter were to be killed. Her heart broke in two, not only for her own imagined self, but also for those two poor girls, and their undoubtedly distraught parents.

Wendy made herself a cup of tea. She sat on the sofa in the lounge, with the television on, not really watching it. She was staring at the screen, but her brain refused to register what it was seeing. Instead, the image playing through in her head was of that night almost twenty-two years ago now, when all of her own friends had been murdered.

She could remember it like it was yesterday. She had been seventeen, the same age that Helen was now. She had been dancing at the Halloween party, held annually in the town hall. This was a long time ago now, back in nineteen-sixty-two, so things were a lot different back then. Everything was much calmer, more reserved. Everybody was just out to dance and have a good time. Sure, there was still alcohol, but nobody was out there trying to get wasted, not like the kids did nowadays.

Wendy had gone to the party with her friends – Carol and Janet. They had arranged to meet some boys there. Their names escaped her now, but she seemed to recall one of them being named Frank. Anyway, those boys never showed up. That was fine by Wendy; she wasn't looking for a date that night anyway. She was quite content just to dance. Rock'n'roll was big news back then. Wendy loved *Cliff Richard* and *Elvis Presley*, and it was their songs which made up the majority of the soundtrack that evening.

The hall had been decorated in a suitable spooky manner. Streamers and balloons were taped to the walls. Papier-mâché spiders, slathered in black poster paint, hung from the ceiling on string. Carboard cut-outs adorned the windows – ghosts and bats and spiders in webs. A carboard skeleton hung over the bar, each individual bone attached to the next with a split pin, so that they could be manoeuvred into any given position. The centrepiece of each table was a jack-o'-lantern, macabre faces carved into the flesh of each pumpkin.

Many of the partygoers were dressed in costumes. Some wore flimsy plastic masks of Dracula and Frankenstein's monster. Others had their faces painted, creepy clowns and spooky skeletons.

Wendy herself had decided not to dress up. Instead, she wore a blue dress, with bright blue eye shadow, and she curled her hair so as to distinguish herself from her usual look. Carol and Janet had gone for a similar tactic; no fancy dress, just an outfit dissimilar enough to their usual attire that it seemed as if they'd made an effort.

But that was all for nothing anyway; the boys hadn't shown up, and both Carol and Janet would be dead before the evening was concluded.

The authorities could've done something. They *should've* done something. They must've known the danger that George Milton posed to the general public. They should've done something to stop him. They should've prevented him from escaping in the first *fucking* place.

Milton was already forty-two on the night of the massacre. He'd been locked up for more than a decade, for the vicious kidnapping, rape and murder of seven women in London. He'd snatched them from the streets and taken them to his home, where he'd kept them locked up in his cellar. When they finally caught him, he was deemed insane on account of how he went on to sexually assault the victims after they had expired – including one woman whose corpse he continued to rape even as the flesh began to rot from her bones – and so was spared the death penalty (oh, how Wendy wished they'd just hung the son-of-a-bitch).

They'd have executed him after the massacre, for sure. But there was no need; Wendy had taken care of that for them.

Nobody knew *how* exactly, but Milton had managed to escape the loony bin to which he'd been committed. This particular asylum had been built in 1914, on the outskirts of Oakhill. None of the town's residents had been happy about this at first, but when nothing of any concern happened, they just seemed to forget that it even existed. Even as she was growing up, Wendy wasn't really aware of its presence.

She knew it was there, of course, but nobody ever really talked about the place.

Milton had approached the town hall from the rear. It was here that he found his first victims. Wendy couldn't recall their names – she wasn't sure that she'd ever known them – but she knew that it was a boy and a girl, both just a little older than she was. They'd gone out the back for some privacy. She couldn't be sure, but she assumed they'd gone to make love. Milton had crept up on them – he must have; they couldn't possibly have been aware of his presence – and slashed their throats.

He'd entered the building then, through the rear fire escape. He'd killed two people in the back room, and another in the kitchen. No doubt they were screaming as he sliced them to ribbons, terrified and in floods of pain. But nobody heard them over the deafening music.

He'd attacked a woman in the bathroom, smashing her head against the mirror until the glass shattered, the shards carving through her face. This act of aggression hadn't killed her though; her death came as he penetrated her with the blade of his knife, entering her between her thighs, and dragging the blade upwards, opening her stomach, and spilling the grizzly contents.

It mustn't have been long after that, when Carol had gone to use the bathroom and found the woman's eviscerated carcass. She'd tried to run, but Milton had caught her, stabbing her in the back more than a dozen times. Wendy wanted to believe that Carol would've tried to warn them of the impending danger, had she not been killed so soon. That was the sort of thing Carol would've done. She was a good friend. She wouldn't have left the others there to fend for themselves. Unlike the authorities, she would've tried to do something.

Wendy could still picture the grief-stricken look on Janet's face, when they'd come across Carol's butchered corpse, the back of her dress as ragged as the flesh beneath, the material saturated with blood, her blonde hair stained a carminic red. Wendy remembered the sense of abject terror she'd felt as her eyes fell upon the gory remains. It felt like a punch to the gut. Wendy felt it now, as if it were happening again, right before her eyes. She'd sobbed over Carol's body, screaming, shaking her shoulders, begging her to wake up. Begging her to not be dead. She only stopped when Janet pulled her away, screaming for them to *get the fuck out of there.*

They'd ran back to the hall, to warn the others.

But it was already too late.

Milton had beaten them there.

There were already half a dozen dead bodies littering the hall. People were running, screaming, blood leaking from their bodies. The corpse of a boy slumped across one of the tables, the skin of his face hacked apart, the bone visible beneath. Milton had forced a girl onto one of the other tables, and was now straddling her. Her thrashing arms knocked the jack-o'-lantern from the table, the pumpkin splitting, juices splattering as it hit the solid wooden floor. Milton had driven the point of his knife into the girls left eye socket. He was twisting the blade, scooping out the mangled ocular organ.

Janet had screamed. Wendy grabbed her by the arm and tried to drag her towards the exit. But Janet was frozen to the spot, her petrified body as solid as a statue. It was as if her feet were nailed to the floor, her body unmoving. Only when Milton had begun to stalk towards them did Janet seem to snap out of that trance. They turned and they ran.

But Milton was like a man possessed. Despite his age, he was still quick. Wendy could feel her feet slipping beneath her, the soles of her shoes unable to grip the blood-slicked floor. Milton drove his knife into Janet's back. The force of the impact knocked both her and Wendy off their feet. Wendy had quickly scrambled up to her knees. She reached for Janet, wanting to pull her out of harm's way. But Milton had swung for her then. She raised her arms in defence. She could still feel the pain of the blade as it sliced through the meat of her palm, bouncing from the metatarsal bones below.

Wendy still had that scar. She balled her fist and dug her fingernails into the tender flesh, just to remind herself of the pain she'd felt that evening. It was nothing compared to the pain the others had felt. At least she'd survived.

Back in the hall all those years ago, Wendy could remember watching as Milton stabbed Janet over and over and over again, blood splashing over her each time that he tore the blade free. And then he was standing over Wendy herself. She was on her back, clutching at the terrible gash inflicted to her hand, trying to prevent the fluids escaping her body.

Milton was smiling. Wendy could picture his blood-spattered face, as clear as day. His eyes were black, beset by deep wrinkles. Harsh crevices furrowed his brow. His black hair was mottled grey, as was the beard that lined his chin. His wide grin exposed his rotten teeth, many of them already chipped, or missing entirely.

He licked his lips, salivating at the thought of carving through Wendy's flesh.

At least, that's what she imagined he was thinking.

He was looking down at her, like a lion might look down at a wounded gazelle, just letting it know that it was the victor, and that any suffering it had endured would soon be over. Her heart racing, she felt helpless. But she couldn't let him win, not so easily. She couldn't let him get away with the things he'd done to her friends. He was standing over her, confident, over-zealous. He must've thought she was weak. He must've thought that she'd just lie there, and take whatever she had coming, praying to God for the sweet release of death. He must've thought she wouldn't fight back.

But Wendy wanted to survive. She *had* to survive.

She drove her foot upward, between his legs, planting her heel deep into his groin. She must've kicked him hard enough to rupture a testicle.

Milton doubled over, gasping for air. He dropped the knife.

Wendy took the opportunity to climb back to her feet. Slipping in the blood, she struggled to gain purchase. But then she was up, running for the door once again, desperate to leave that hall of horrors behind her.

Milton gave chase. He was right behind her, the sour stench of his breath breathing down her neck. He slammed into Wendy, his shoulder crashing through her spine. Wendy hit the floor hard, the air knocked from her lungs, her lower lip splitting on impact. She could still taste the blood on her tongue. The taste, bitter and metallic.

Wendy had rolled to her back, ready to fight Milton once more. But he was already on top of her, his massive weight crushing her ribs into oblivion. He wrapped his hands around her neck and squeezed, crushing her trachea, cutting off the supply of oxygen. Her lungs burned in her chest. Her hands groped out to the sides, her fingers scrambling for anything she might be able to use as a weapon.

They found their way to an empty beer bottle. Somebody must've knocked it over from one of the tables as they'd made their hasty escape. Wendy grabbed it and swung with all her might. The bottle hit Milton on the back of his head, and burst in an explosion of broken glass, the shards digging into his scalp.

His grip loosened enough for Wendy to break free. She raised her knees, tucking them up between the two of them. She pushed, knocking Milton aside, his feet going out from under him.

Wendy rolled to her front. Her eyes scanned her surroundings. She needed a weapon.

A scarecrow stood by the door, bound to a wooden cross, as if it had been crucified. Its straw body spilled from the tattered shirt it wore so elegantly. Its head slumped to one side, a twisted grin painted onto the fabric of the burlap sack. At its feet, straw had been scattered on the floor. More jack-o'-lanterns smiled menacingly at Wendy, almost as if they wanted her dead, so they could feast on her soul. A log sat on its side, cut from the trunk of some thick oak. An axe had been embedded into the wood.

Wendy hurried. She wrapped her hands around the handle of the axe and pulled. It was stuck tight. She placed her foot onto the log, right next to where the head of the axe had been implanted, and pulled once more. She gritted her teeth and screamed.

The axe came loose.

Milton was back to his feet. He charged at Wendy.

She turned and swung the axe.

The blade slammed into the side of Milton's neck, splitting his arteries wide open. Blood gushed from the wound, cascading down the front of his shirt, soaking it crimson. Wendy pulled the blade away, finding that it came much easier from Milton's neck than it had done from the log.

Milton stood firm, gore oozing over his lips, drooling down his chin. Blood spurted from the ruined blood vessels.

Breathing heavy, Wendy raised the axe once more. She swung it again, planting it directly into the same spot where it had landed before. This time, Milton's neck crunched. Wendy wasn't sure whether this was his tendons cracking, or whether she'd hit bone. Whatever it was, the blow was enough to knock Milton off his feet.

He clamped his hands onto his throat, trying in vain to stop the flow of blood. But it was useless; the wound was so deep that his head was barely hanging on.

Might as well remove it entirely.

Wendy swung the axe overhead, bringing it down on the front of Milton's neck. The force of the blade slamming into his hands obliterated the bones within. Two of his fingers were severed entirely.

Wendy raised the axe again, and chopped once more. Over and over, she repeated the process – chop, chop, chop, chop, chop – until Milton's head finally came loose, separated from his body, a widening pool of ichor spreading from his body.

The nightmare was over.

The police had arrived just a few moments later.

Fat lot of good they were now.

Since then, the town's annual party had effectively been banned. It wasn't illegal to throw a party, of course, but the town would no longer officially sanction one, out of respect for the victims. That could only be a good thing.

After that night, Wendy had pretty much been scared of everything. She was even scared of her own shadow. That was over twenty years ago now; it would be twenty-two years in four days' time, to be precise – on Halloween night. A lot had happened between then and now. But her anxiety had never relinquished its stranglehold on her. If anything, it had gotten worse since Helen had been born.

She loved that little girl so much; she wouldn't be able to cope if anything were ever to happen to her.

It was just the two of them now; Helen's father had left a few years after she'd been born. He'd had an affair with one of his co-workers, and had since moved to the other end of the country.

Good riddance to bad rubbish, as far as Wendy was concerned. It was hard for Helen, of course, but she was strong; stronger than Wendy herself, perhaps. Nothing could ever break her. It was this knowledge that gave Wendy some comfort, knowing that Helen was sensible enough to run should danger ever present itself. Wendy had always tried to allow Helen that freedom, to be a child, to be a teenager, to live her life however she saw fit.

Wendy's own life now consisted only of her house, the doctor's surgery (where she worked as a receptionist, part time), and her Friday night book club. But even book club wouldn't be the same now. Sandra most certainly wouldn't be there – not for a while, at least.

Helen would be okay. Nothing was going to happen to her.

Wendy closed her eyes and tried her hardest to forget the past.

--- --- --- --- --- --- --- --- --- --- --- ---

Times have changed, and not for the better. The world isn't like it used to be. Parents used to be able to allow their children out to play on the streets, without fear that they might be kidnapped or murdered. Now, we do not know what monsters lurk around each corner. Films such as Night Of The Demon *and* The Slayer *paint the villain as some kind of horrifying, supernatural entity. But they are not. The monsters we ought to fear are real men, made of flesh and blood, driven beyond the brink of insanity. These so-called 'video nasties' can only serve to play a part in this ensuing epidemic of madness.*

Gary Smart, conservative MP and

campaigner against social liberalism

Chapter Four:

The Cannibal Man

Helen found herself glad when the final bell rang out through the college hallways, allowing her to escape the musty classroom, out into the cool, fresh air of the afternoon.

She couldn't wait to get out of there. The whole place felt claustrophobic, like something was squeezing her ribs, as if a boa constrictor had wrapped itself around her torso, and was waiting for her to suffocate so it could consume her whole.

Helen pulled on her coat, and wrapped her scarf around her neck, before exiting the building, scooting down the steps and into the middle of the lawn. She needed to wait for Lorraine and Anna – they always walked home together – but she really couldn't wait inside. She needed to be out in the open, without that restrictive presence looming over her.

She needed to be able to breathe.

It was a strange feeling, like nothing she'd ever felt before. She wasn't normally one to worry. But now, a peculiar anxiety bubbled in the pit of her stomach. Something told her that this just wasn't right. Amy and Tina were dead. From what she'd heard, they'd been brutally murdered. Helen hadn't known Tina all too well, but she and Amy used to be good friends a few years back. As so often happens, as kids grow up and are forced to navigate that treacherous path through their teenage years, the two of them had drifted apart. They still spoke occasionally, whenever they passed in the college halls, or when they just so happened to bump into each other while they were out shopping, or whatever. They were friendly, but truth be told, they weren't really *friends* anymore.

But that didn't stop Helen's heart from hammering the inside of her ribcage, making her limbs feel numb.

What had Amy done to deserve this? What had *either* of them done?

Two more news vans had now joined the ITN van parked outside the college. Cameras had been set up and reports had been recorded. The reporters had tried to coax interviews out of as many of the students as they could, stopping them as they came and went, shoving microphones into their faces. Some of the students had been glad to voice their opinions on what had happened, and what they thought of Amy and Tina, somehow thinking that they were going to be famous. Helen had done her best to avoid the journalists, not wanting to talk to *them* about what she was feeling right now. She knew that if anybody were to ask her how she was feeling, she would almost certainly break down into floods of tears. Nobody needed to see that – least of all the great British public, who would no doubt be glued to their televisions tonight, gagging for any morsels of gossip about the two butchered teenagers.

Some of the girls' close friends were currently sitting on the edge of the lawn, huddled together, crying for their lost acquaintances. Helen felt bad for them. But most of all, she just felt glad that this wasn't her. She didn't think she could cope with the devastation right now.

"Hey!" said a voice, closer than Helen believed anybody could possibly have been. "How's it going?"

Helen jumped out of her skin. She whirled around to see who it was that had so deviously sneaked up on her.

It was Mark.

Relief flooded Helen's body. "Jesus Christ!" she exclaimed, her heart thundering even harder now. "You scared the shit out of me!"

Mark chuckled. His smile was perfect. "Sorry," he said. "That wasn't my intention."

"Yeah? Well… intended or not, I think I just wet myself."

Mark laughed again, louder this time. But then his face turned more solemn. "Are you okay? I guess you've heard about what happened."

Helen nodded. "Yeah, I heard. I think that's why I'm so jumpy."

Mark placed his hand on Helen's shoulder, squeezing it gently. "It's okay, you know? There's nothing for you to worry about. I'm here for you, if you need me."

Helen had never intended to fall for Mark. She'd known him for years, and never had romance figured into the equation between them. Of course, for most of the time she'd known him, she'd been dating Kevin, so the possibility of anything happening between Mark and herself had always been off the table. But she and Kevin were no longer together. That meant there was an opening in her life, one which Mark seemed quite keen to fill. But it had only been two months since she'd broken it off with Kevin. That was far too soon, wasn't it?

But then again, Mark was a really nice guy. He was tall and handsome and intelligent and funny. Helen really liked him. He wouldn't wait for *her* forever, would he? What if somebody else came along – somebody smarter and prettier than Helen was – and whisked him away from her?

She ought to do something, to make sure that didn't happen.

"I know," said Helen, forcing herself to smile, hoping that in doing so, she might just force herself to *actually* be happy. "I just feel like something isn't right, you know? I mean, how is this fair? Why did they have to die?"

Mark shrugged his shoulders, his eyebrows raised. "I don't know. It's a cruel world we live in these days, and there are some serious psychos out there. I'm just glad it wasn't anybody I care about."

"You don't care about them?" said Helen, referring to Amy and Tina, and already knowing that wasn't what Mark had meant.

"Of course I care. But, you know, I'm just glad it wasn't anybody I care about more." He paused for a second, before adding: "Like you, for example."

Helen smiled, finding that she was already feeling much better. “Thanks. I guess.”

They were both laughing then.

Lorraine approached Helen from behind, arm in arm with Chris. “Well, well, well,” she said. “What do we have here then?” Her wide smile almost looked demented. She knew how Helen felt about Mark – exactly the same way he felt about her. “You two look like you’re having fun!”

Helen rolled her eyes. “We were just talking, for Christ’s sake.”

“Oh, sure. Just talking. Right. Whatever.” Lorraine grinned sarcastically.

Anna and Ryan were there too. Anna had her hands folded across her chest. “We were looking for you inside,” said Anna. “You in a rush to get home or something?”

“No,” said Helen. “I’ve just had enough of this place. I felt like I couldn’t breathe in there. I think the whole day has just gotten to me.”

“Ugghh…” spat Lorraine. “Tell me about it. I just had economics. I swear to God, Mr. Peterson kept trying to look at my tits out the corner of his eye. He does it all the time. He thinks I don’t notice, but I do.”

“Come off it,” said Chris, snorting a laugh. “You love the attention!”

“I’m not saying that I don’t,” laughed Lorraine. “But not off *that* dirty old pervert!”

“Look,” interjected Ryan, “we already know how much of a slut Lorraine is, so how about we get just out of here?”

Lorraine frowned at Ryan, who only offered a wink in return.

“Yeah, come on,” said Chris. “Let’s get moving.”

The six of them crossed the lawn, leaving the college building – as well as the creepy Halloween decorations, which only now did Helen begin to consider might’ve been partly to blame for the anxiety she was feeling – far behind them. As soon as they were out of the gates, Anna pulled out her cigarettes and offered them around.

"Hold up," said Ryan, his hand raised. "I've got something even better." He shrugged his rucksack off of his shoulder – he'd been using only one strap – and reached inside. When he withdrew his hand, with it he pulled a small Altoids mint tin. He popped open the tin and took out a joint.

"Ooh, nice," said Lorraine, grinning like a maniac.

"Not for me thank you," said Helen.

"Don't be so boring," scoffed Anna.

Helen raised a single eyebrow. "Boring? Do you know what would happen to me if my mom knew I'd been smoking weed? You know what she's like! She'd flip out if she knew I'd been smoking cigarettes. If she thought I was taking drugs, she'd probably murder me!" Helen had smoked weed before, as well as having taken the odd pill here and there. But that had only been at parties, when she knew that either the effects would have worn off by the time she got home, or that her mother would already be asleep by the time she walked in through the front door.

Ryan removed the lit joint from between his lips and exhaled a huge plume of white smoke. "Yeah. And we don't need any more funerals to attend, right?"

Helen frowned. "You're *not even* funny."

Ryan grinned a shit-eating grin.

"Yeah," said Lorraine, as she took the joint from Ryan and took a long, deep drag. "You're not *funny*, Ryan. You're fucking *hilarious*!"

"Don't encourage him," sighed Helen, shaking her head.

Lorraine laughed. She passed the joint to Chris, who took a drag, then passed it to Anna, who took a drag and offered it to Mark.

Mark held his hands up in defence. "No thank you," he said. "I've got football later. I can't be turning up to training stoned. They'll kick me off the team."

"Suit yourself," said Ryan, taking the joint back.

Helen smiled at Mark, knowing that he didn't really care about playing football stoned, and that he'd only declined the weed so that she wouldn't be the only one not partaking. It was just another thing to make her like him even more. He really cared about her.

"Anyway," Ryan continued, as he took another deep toke on the joint, "this is the last of my weed. I just need to drop in and see Russ on the way past."

"Oh," said Helen, her eyebrows raised, mostly in mock surprise. "Is he dealing again now?"

"He never stopped."

Helen wasn't exactly Russ' biggest fan. He was about six or seven years older than they were. He'd dropped out of school at the age of fourteen, hoping to pursue a career as a musician. He played bass in a heavy metal band – they were called 'The Devil Pigs', or something stupid like that. The biggest problem they had, was that they fucking sucked. Their career hadn't taken off, of course, and they'd split up a year or so later. Russ hadn't even been sixteen at the time. His parents had tried to get him back into school, but apparently the school had refused to take him. They'd allegedly reached capacity. He'd been offered a place at a school in a neighbouring town, but his parents just couldn't be bothered to take him. Since then, he'd made his money selling marijuana, and running the video shop that his uncle owned (his uncle himself being in prison for dealing). "I thought his parents said that if the police had to bring him home one more time, they'd kick his worthless ass out."

"They did," laughed Ryan. "I guess that just hasn't happened yet. Besides, his mom doesn't know this, but his dad is actually his best customer!"

Laughing, they cut through an alleyway at the back of the street, emerging onto the road that led into the shopping complex.

There were a dozen shops in the complex. All the usual suspects were present and correct – butcher, greengrocer, newsagent, baker, barbershop. A Chinese takeaway stood on the corner, Helen's favourite place to get food at the weekend. The video shop stood opposite. An acrylic sign – the corners of the plastic chipped away – stretched the entre width of the storefront, the name 'VIDEO MAGIC' having faded in the sunlight. Two fluorescent tubes were mounted behind the sign, one of which blinked on and off repeatedly. The whole shop could do with a makeover, Helen often thought.

A bell rang as the six of them entered the shop, drawing Russ' attention from behind the counter. "Hey!" he called, oozing with enthusiasm, no doubt founded on the fact that he knew he was about to make some money. "How's it going?"

The shop smelled funny. It *always* smelled funny. It smelled old. It was musty, as if the walls were drenched in damp. In all actuality, it was highly probable that this was the case. It also didn't help that customers were allowed to smoke in there. Cigarette smoke got into everything, penetrating every nook and cranny, the scent lingering. Helen herself smoked, of course, although she never really considered herself to be a 'smoker' – there had to be some minimum daily quota for that title, a number she would surely fall short of. So, it wasn't as if she had anything against smokers, but the stale smell of dirty ashtrays was far from pleasant.

"I'm good," said Ryan, leading the group towards the counter. "And yourself?"

"Never better," smirked Russ. He had long, greasy hair, all the way down to his shoulders. It was wavy, but it clung to the sides of his head, allowing his ears to poke through at the sides. His face was littered with zits, like maybe he never washed. He wore glasses with thick lenses, that magnified his eyes to twice their usual size.

The shop itself was empty, no other customers perused the shelves. Sometimes, especially on a Friday or Saturday night, the place could be packed. But right now, at two-fifty-five on a Monday afternoon, nobody was looking to rent a movie. Shelves lined the two side walls, top to bottom, plastic units affixed side by side, which allowed the tapes stored there to be displayed at a slight angle, so that both the spine and part of the cover were always visible. A number of smaller units occupied the middle of the shop floor, each one stacked with videos. Small signs pinned to the shelves denoted the genre of film stored there – Family, Action, Comedy, Sports, Horror.

"So," said Ryan, leaning onto the counter. "You got any weed for sale?"

"Of course," said Russ. "How much do you want?"

"Half an ounce?"

"Coming right up!"

Russ disappeared into the small room at the back of the shop. Helen turned to look around the shop. Posters had been taped to the window, advertising films such as *Flashdance* and *Rocky III*. A standee for *Return Of The Jedi* took pride of place next to the door, Darth Vader looming over Princess Leia and Luke Skywalker, the latter with his lightsabre at the ready.

"So," said Russ, as he re-emerged from the back room. "I heard about those two girls getting killed. Some nasty shit, right?"

"Yeah," said Ryan, handing Russ a bundle of cash in return for his drugs, unable to hide his smirk. "Sounds like they got butchered."

"What do you mean?" asked Lorraine. "I thought nobody knew what happened to them."

"Nobody knows for sure," agreed Ryan. "But I heard that one of them got their brains drilled out of their skull!"

The thought repulsed Helen. Why would anybody do such a thing? And why did Ryan sound so *happy* about it? Did he not understand that these were real people, with real families? Nobody deserved to have their life taken in such a way.

"No shit!" said Russ. "Sounds like there's a 'driller killer' on the loose!"

"A 'driller killer'?" scoffed Anna, confused.

"Yeah. Like in the film. You know? *The Driller Killer*? The video nasty?"

"I don't think I've seen that one," said Chris.

"Oh, man!" said Russ, growing all the more excited. "You *need* to watch it! It's about this guy who just goes crazy, then starts running around murdering people with an electric drill."

Was that what happened to Amy and Tina? wandered Helen. Did somebody just go crazy, and kill them all because they were in the wrong place at the wrong time? That couldn't be it. There had to be more of a reason than that. Chris had said earlier that they believed it was a burglary gone wrong. At least that was *some kind* of a reason; not a *good* reason, but a reason, nevertheless. Helen decided she'd stick with believing that, at least for the time being.

"Sounds gross," said Anna, referring to the film.

"Sounds amazing!" said Ryan, on the verge of hysterics.

"You wanna borrow it?" asked Russ.

"Do you have it?"

Russ frowned, his eyebrows cocked as if this were the stupidest question he'd ever been asked. "What do you take me for? Of course I have it!"

"I thought the video nasties were banned," said Helen, the statement almost meant as a question.

"They are," said Russ, ducking down behind the counter, "that's why I keep them down here, out of sight, and I only rent them out when I'm sure the pigs aren't around, to people I can be sure aren't gonna rat me out." When he stood back up, he did so with a large cardboard box in his arms. He dropped the box onto the counter and pulled open the flaps.

Ryan and Chris both stared into the box, wide eyed, as if they'd just stumbled upon the holy grail. Thankfully – not that it was any of her business, not yet anyway – Mark wasn't quite so enthralled with contents of the box. Despite how dumb both Chris and Ryan were acting, Helen couldn't help but feel her curiosity piqued. She stepped forward to take a closer look.

Video tapes had been stacked inside the box, the spines facing upward so that the titles were visible. Some she recognised – such as *I Spit On Your Grave* and *The Evil Dead* – while others, she didn't – like *Madhouse* and *Absurd*, and the awesomely titled *Mardi Gras Massacre*.

Russ began to pull the videos from the box, distributing them amongst the group for all to see.

Lorraine shuffled through a stack of tapes, reeling off the titles – "*Cannibal. Cannibals. Cannibal Ferox. Cannibal Terror. Cannibal*

Holocaust. Prisoner Of The Cannibal God. Wow… that's a lot of cannibals."

"You should probably add *Eaten Alive* and *Deep River Savages* to that pile," said Russ, smiling ecstatically, like a kid in a candy store.

"How about *The Cannibal Man*?" asked Anna, displaying the tape she was currently holding for the others to see.

Russ wrinkled his nose and shook his head. "Nah. That one's not really a cannibal film."

"Well," said Lorraine, eyebrows raised. "You sure seem to know a lot about cannibal films."

"That's 'cause he *is* the 'cannibal man'," laughed Ryan.

"Ah," Russ said, as he pulled another tape from the box. He handed it to Chris. "Here it is – *The Driller Killer*."

Lorraine peered over Chris' shoulder, screwing her face up at the sight of the grizzly cover art. "Well, that's gross," she said.

"Let me see," said Helen, not sure why she even wanted to look.

Chris handed her the tape. The image on the front was a photo – presumably a still from the movie itself – of a man, screaming in agony, a drill bit driving through his forehead, blood cascading down his face. This picture, although not particularly gruesome, did still manage to turn her stomach. "Very nice," she said sarcastically, handing the tape back to Chris.

"You want anything else?" asked Russ, waving his hands over the tapes now scattered on the counter.

"Hold up," said Chris, having pulled open the case of the video he held in his hands. "What's this? Seriously?"

"What?"

"This is Betamax. I don't have a Betamax player!"

"Really?" Russ scanned the others, one eyebrow raised, making it painfully clear that he couldn't quite believe what he was hearing. "You want *VHS*? Shit, man – the quality of Betamax is *so much* better!"

"Is that right? I bet you've got copies of every single film in this shop on VHS, and I bet you've got less than half on Betamax."

"So? What's your point?"

"*Nobody* wants Betamax!"

Russ burst into laughter. "Ha! Yeah, right! Trust me; in just a few years' time, *everybody* will be watching Betamax. VHS will be dead!"

Chris rolled his eyes. "Yeah. We'll see."

Russ dug around in the box for a moment, then pulled out another tape, the case identical to the one which Chris was already holding. "Here," he said, swapping the tapes over. "VHS. Happy now?"

"Very."

"Good."

"Hey," said Ryan, waving a hand in front of Russ' face, as if he were a jealous child who had been painfully ignored. "Can I borrow this one?" He was holding a copy of a film called *Anthropophagous*. The cover showed a man with a bad case of eczema on his face, blood dribbling down his chin from where he had, presumably, just taken a bite from… what? An undercooked steak perhaps. *Not likely*, thought Helen, amusing herself.

"Oh yeah," said Russ. "That's a good one! The guy cuts open a pregnant woman's belly and eats her baby!"

"That's fucking disgusting!" said Lorraine.

"Yeah," agreed Anna. "What's wrong with you? Why would you want to watch shit like that?"

"Because it's funny!" laughed Ryan, the weed he'd smoked apparently giving him the giggles.

Helen sighed. "Anyway," she said, drawing the word out so that nobody could fail to notice that she was talking. "If we're done here, we really need to get going."

"Yeah," said Mark. "As fun as this has been, I've gotta get home and get ready for training."

"Are we still goin' into town?" asked Lorraine, her question directed towards Helen.

"Yeah," Helen replied. "Just so long as we hurry up. I need to pop home first, to drop off my stuff."

"Alright, alright. Let's get going."

"Okay," said Russ, packing his video nasties back into the box from which they'd came. "Enjoy your films. And, do me a favour; don't tell anybody where you got them from. And don't turn into a bunch of homicidal maniacs, okay?"

Chris snorted a laugh. "What do you mean?"

"Well," said Russ. "Those girls that died, if one of them really did have her head *drilled* open, well then, maybe the killer really was inspired by *The Driller Killer*. Maybe the politicians are right. Maybe these films *can* drive people insane."

"Jesus, Russ," snarled Lorraine. "Can you *not* say shit like that, maybe? I don't want a serial killer for a boyfriend."

"I'm just saying, is all," said Russ, his hands raised, palms forward in surrender. "It certainly sounds like this killer tried to recreate a scene from a video nasty. Next thing you know, we'll have our very own *Leatherface* running around, chopping people up with a chainsaw."

"Fuck," said Chris. "Let's hope not."

"Alright," said Ryan, ending the conversation, "we're off. I'll see you later, okay?"

"Right you are," said Russ. "And don't forget, if the police ask, you didn't get those videos from me."

"You got it."

Helen was glad to be outside once more, the refreshing autumn air filling her lungs. Only now that she was outside did she realise just how claustrophobic and oppressive the video shop had been.

Then again, perhaps it was just the excessive talk of death and murder that was weighing her down.

--- --- --- --- --- --- --- --- --- --- --- ---

These movies inspire me. They've inspired an entire generation. This is all I want to do. This is my life. I love the blood and the guts. I love to cut people's heads off. I love to slice them open and pull their insides out, like a string of bloody sausages. But none of it is real, man! It's all make-believe! I'm a filmmaker. I'm like a magician – what you see on screen is all a trick. And these kids are smart enough to see through the illusion and enjoy it for what it is. Do you really think people believe that Olga Karlatos actually had her eyeball impaled on a wooden splinter in Zombie Flesh Eaters*? No – they don't. We all know it isn't real. These films pose zero threat to anybody.*

Adam Chambers, independent

filmmaker and horror movie fanatic

CHAPTER FIVE:

PRANKS

"Seriously?" Helen's mother scolded her. "One of your friends was just murdered, and you want to go out roaming the streets?"

Wendy – Helen's mother – had always been overprotective. Helen got it; she'd been through some serious shit. But that was a long time ago. Times had changed. Nobody was out there now, stalking the streets, looking for victims. What had happened to Amy and Tina was a tragedy, but there was no reason to think that there was some sort of mass murderer on the loose.

"Amy was hardly my friend, Mom," came Helen's reply, one which she almost instantly regretted.

Helen's mother raised her eyebrows. "She *used* to be your *best* friend!"

Helen looked at the ground, knowing that she didn't mean it to come out quite as callously as it had. "I know, I know. I didn't mean that. But, that was in the past. Things change. *People* change. Nothing's going to happen to me. You have to trust me."

"It's not *you* that I don't trust – it's everybody else."

"But that's hardly fair on me, is it?" scoffed Helen, rolling her eyes.

Her mother sighed, shaking her head, no reasonable answer to give. "Well, where exactly is it you plan on going?"

"Just into town. Nowhere I haven't been a million times before." Helen was starting to feel as if she was going over the same thing, over and over again.

"But not when there's been a killer on the loose, Helen!"

"You're worrying about nothing!"

Helen knew this wasn't exactly true. There was *something* to worry about – *somebody* had killed Amy and Tina. There *was* a murderer on the loose, but, so far, there had been no suggestion that this was a serial killer. The police had confirmed that they believed this to be an isolated incident. And besides, even if this was a serial killer, what were the chances of Helen becoming their next victim?

Her mother sighed once again. "Well," she said, her hands on her hips as if there was no chance of her admitting defeat. "Will you be home before it gets dark?"

Helen scoffed a laugh. "I doubt it, no. It'll be dark in, like, an hour!" It was already nearly four-thirty, and the nights were drawing in earlier now, as winter grew nearer. "I'm not going to be alone. I'll be with Lorraine and Anna. We'll look after each other."

"Amy wasn't alone either, but she *and* her friend still managed to get killed."

"Mom. Please…" Helen hated talking to her mother about that terrible night, all those years ago, before she was even born. But sometimes, especially when her mother wanted to treat Helen like some kind of a victim, she *had* to bring it up. "This isn't like what happened to you. George Milton is dead. You killed him! He's not coming back. He's not out there, waiting to kill me."

"I know that, Helen!" screamed her mother, her cheeks turning a furious shade of purple. Although the colour remained in her cheeks, she took a breath and calmed her voice. "I was there, remember? I'm the one that had to cut his head off with an axe! He killed my friends. I know it wasn't him that killed those two poor girls. But *somebody* killed them. That same *somebody* could be out there, right now, waiting to kill *you*!"

"I'm not going to be just some other victim, Mom. You don't need to worry."

"But I *do* worry, Helen," said her mother, a tone of sadness now ebbing its way into her voice. "I can't lose you, Helen. I just *can't*."

Helen smiled, sympathetically. "You won't, Mom. I'm not going anywhere. But you have to let me live my life. You can't wrap me in bubble-wrap, and you can't lock me up in this house. I can look after myself."

Helen's mother nodded, admitting defeat, her white flag waving. "I know you can. I just… God… Everything's just so hard nowadays."

Helen nodded, understanding. "I know. I get it. What happened to you and your friends was absolutely terrible. But that was a long time ago. So much has changed. This isn't the same thing."

Her mother nodded in return. "I killed George Milton. I know that. I *know* he's dead. I'm not crazy, I *know* this isn't him. But for years afterwards, I used to feel like people were watching me, talking about me behind my back. I was constantly on edge. I used to imagine somebody killing me, revenge for what I'd done to Milton."

Helen could feel herself frowning. Her mother had never told her this before. She'd gone into fairly vivid detail about everything that had happened that night, but she'd never really spoken about what had happened in the immediate aftermath. The look on her mother's face almost seemed to suggest that she herself had forgotten these details. Perhaps the new murders had dredged these memories up. "Why would anybody do that?" asked Helen. "George Milton was a psychopath. He deserved to die."

Helen's mother nodded, fighting back the tears that threatened to spill down her cheeks. "It was an irrational fear, of course. But, to my mind, it was entirely possible that *anybody* could've been a psycho, too. What if somebody idolized him, and wanted to finish what he had started? Or what if some long-lost family member came crawling out of the woodwork, seeking redemption?"

Helen couldn't help but chuckle, despite knowing that her mother was entirely serious. "That sounds like the plot of some God-awful horror movie."

Her mother laughed, no doubt understanding the absurdity of what she was suggesting. It was a nice sound to hear. "Yes," her mother agreed. "And I *detest* horror movies!"

Helen was still laughing. She pushed in close to her mother and wrapped her arms around her waist, squeezing her tightly. She loved her mother, truly. Sure, life wasn't easy when your only parent was constantly on the brink of a nervous breakdown. But that was beyond her control; Helen couldn't hold that against her. "Honestly, Mom," Helen said, "I'll be okay. I'm almost an adult, and I know not to talk to strangers."

Her mother laughed again. "I know. And I trust you. Just promise you'll be safe, okay?"

"I will. Believe me, I have no intention of getting myself killed."

Her mother snorted a semi-laugh as she sniffed back her tears. "I'm very glad to hear that."

—

The high street was pretty much dead by the time Helen, Lorraine, and Anna had arrived there. It was cold out, and many of the shops had already started to close. As such, only a handful of people still seemed to be lingering.

The three girls had planned to go shopping for clothes, but Anna had insisted that she needed to pick up the new *Sheena Easton* album, so they headed to the record store first, before it too closed for the night.

There were no independent record stores in town – which, of course, would've been Helen's preference – so their only option was the soulless *Our Price* at the end of the street.

A few people mingled around inside the record shop, browsing the LPs and cassettes that lined the shelves. An older gentleman, his glasses clinging precariously onto the tip of his nose, scanned through the top forty. A pair of punks – one with long, greasy hair down to his shoulders, the other with a short Mohican, dyed bright green – were hanging around in the 'rock' section, laughing and snorting loudly, as if the sole purpose for their existence was to be as obnoxious as possible. A group of teenagers that Helen vaguely recognised as attending the same college as her, albeit a year or two ahead, loitered by the entrance, chatting to the girl behind the counter. One of the other girls there giggled hysterically as a boy that Helen assumed was her boyfriend nibbled playfully at her neck.

Anna found the album she was looking for and picked up the cassette. "Ah," she said. "Got it."

"I think I'm gonna get this one," smirked Lorraine, as she held up an LP by the band *Metallica*. The cover showed some horrifying demon, engulfed in the flames of hell. She poked out her index and pinkie fingers, making the devil horns salute, and scrunched her nose into what she apparently considered to be her most terrifying face.

Helen laughed. "Oh, yeah. Sounds great," she said. "Why don't we all go worship the devil?"

Anna stuck out her tongue and shook her hair loose. "Hail Satan!" she giggled.

All three of them were laughing then, until the two punks appeared next to them, almost seeming to materialise out of thin air. "You wanna worship the devil?" said the punk with the greasy hair. His voice was gritty, as if his lungs were full of phlegm. He was wearing a leather jacket, and stonewashed jeans that looked as if they were around two sizes too small, the knees worn through entirely. "You want us to show you how?"

Lorraine raised her eyebrows. "Erm… no thanks," she said. She looked to Helen, rolling her eyes, indicating that this guy was seriously giving her the creeps.

"You sure? We could take you to this place in the forest, just outside of town. There's this alter there. They've performed all sorts of satanic rituals out there."

Helen was already starting to feel uncomfortable. She looked around to see if anybody had noticed them being accosted by these two punks. She considered calling out for help, but then she realised how stupid she'd sound. Besides, Lorraine seemed to have everything under control.

"Seriously? Satanic rituals?" Lorraine scoffed.

The punk nodded, his mohican'ed friend snarling as if he'd just swallowed a wasp. "Tell me – are any of you girls virgins?"

Lorraine raised her eyebrows further still, clearly offended. "What the *fuck*? And why the fuck would I tell *you* that?"

"Sacrificing a virgin is the only sure-fire way of invoking the devil."

Lorraine scoffed, shaking her head. "You sure *you're* not a virgin? I'm surprised your dick still works, being all squashed up in those jeans. Did you steal them off your little sister? I'm surprised you haven't ruptured a testicle."

The punk snorted a laugh. "Don't you worry about that. My cock and balls work just fine. Come with us, and maybe I'll show you first hand."

"Yeah, right. In your dreams."

The punk lowered his head, a frown creasing his forehead. "I don't have dreams," he said, barely any more than whisper. "I only ever have nightmares."

Helen had heard enough. She grabbed Lorraine by the arm and dragged her away. "Come on," she said. "Let's get out of here."

Lorraine smiled back at the two punks. "See ya!"

"If you ever change your mind," the punk called after them as they left, "come and find me, okay? We'll invoke the devil together!"

"Sure. You got it."

The two punks began laughing, exchanging a high-five.

Anna paid for her cassette, and the three of them left the store.

"I can't believe those guys," said Helen, as she snapped pieces of polystyrene from her *McDonald's* cheeseburger box. The way those two punks had spoken to them was still playing on her mind, even now, thirty minutes after the incident had even occurred.

“What guys?” said Lorraine, slurping on her strawberry milkshake. Clearly their interaction with the punks had affected her significantly less so.

The McDonald’s in which they were now sat had been decorated for Halloween. In the window, a carboard cut-out showed Ronald McDonald dressed as Count Dracula, a trio of chicken nuggets adorned with bat wings, flying around his head. Beside him, the Hamburglar’s head had been replaced with a smiling jack-o’-lantern.

“Those two guys in the record shop.”

“The two rock-star wannabes? Forget about them. They were just trying to scare us. You’re not scared are you?”

“No. Not at all. It’s just… I mean… Why would anybody want to worship the devil?”

Lorraine laughed. “I don’t think they *really* worship the devil. I think they were trying to be funny.”

“I agree with Helen,” said Anna, picking the gherkin out of her burger and dropping it into the polystyrene box. “They were giving off some creepy vibes, man.”

Helen nodded her head in agreement.

Lorrain laughed again. “You two are crazy. They were harmless.”

“Yeah, well… I didn’t like it.”

Lorraine snorted back a laugh and took a bite from her own burger.

By the time they had left McDonald’s, all the shops were closed. There would be no clothes shopping for them tonight. They decided to head home.

As they waited at the bus stop, Helen spotted the one thing she’d have hoped never to see again; the two punks were walking along the street, heading in their direction.

“Hey, look!” said Lorraine, clearly having seen them too. “It’s your boyfriend Helen!”

“Stop!” said Helen, more annoyed than she really ought to be.

"There's one for you too Anna," Lorraine giggled. "Maybe you could have a foursome!"

Anna grimaced, screwing up her face. "Ugghh. I couldn't think of anything worse."

Thankfully, the bus turned the corner not a moment too soon.

As the bus pulled up to the bus stop, only then did the two punks notice the three girls they had earlier spoken to in the record shop. "Hey!" called the greasy punk, as he began to run towards them, laughing hysterically. He waved his arm, urging his friend to follow. "Wait there! Come on, come with us into the woods! We want to send you to meet Satan!"

For some reason, Helen's heart was racing. She knew they weren't serious – at least, she *assumed* they weren't – but she suddenly felt extremely scared. Quickly, she hopped up the steps onto the bus. Dropping a handful of change into the tray, the printer buzzed as it presented her with a flimsy paper ticket. Helen tore it off, then Lorraine and Anna both paid.

The driver closed the doors and pulled away from the curb.

The two punks were there then, banging on the door as the bus began to make its way along the high street.

"Don't let them in," Lorraine told the driver.

Thankfully, the driver obliged, and continued along the road.

Laughing, Lorraine stuck up her middle finger, and waved it at the punks.

"Jesus," sighed Helen, dropping into the back seat of the bus. "What's wrong with some people."

"I don't know," said Anna, taking the seat beside her. "There sure are a lot of weirdos out there."

—

“You think that blonde chick fancied me?” said Tommy, running his fingers through his hair, teasing it back over his head. It was getting long now; it’d need trimming soon.

Nigel snorted. “Oh, yeah!” He said, oozing with sarcasm. “She’s probably head over heels in love with you! Just need to make sure your dick still works, right?”

“Yeah, right. I got no problems in that department, trust me.”

“You think they actually believed we worship the devil?” Nigel pondered, scratching the stubble of his scalp.

“Shit… probably. Dumb bitches like that ain’t got a clue.”

Tommy and Nigel were on the bus. For a brief moment, back in town, Tommy had considered the idea that they should’ve chased those girls. They were scared, and it was fucking hilarious. But then, there was no conceivable way for him to know which stop they’d be getting off at. And even if he did, by the time he got there, they’d be long gone. He’d suggested to Nigel that maybe they should go and find somebody else to torment. It wasn’t that he particularly got his kicks from making people scared – he wasn’t a sadist, after all – but so many people saw him and Nigel, and they thought that there was something sinister about them, what with their unusual haircuts and their leather jackets, that it was just funny to him to play up to it. But it was already dark, and the high street was practically deserted. As such, they’d decided that now was probably as good a time as any to head home.

After around twenty minutes on the bus, they arrived at Nigel’s stop. “Alright, man,” he said, as he stood from the seat, steadying himself on the bar that ran along the roof. “I’ll see you tomorrow.”

“Yeah,” said Tommy. “See you tomorrow.”

The brakes of the bus hissed as it pulled up to a stop. Nigel hopped off the bus, as a handful of people got on. Tommy watched through the window as Nigel skulked off into the darkness, his bright green strip of hair the last thing to be swallowed up by the night.

Ten more minutes and the bus arrived at Tommy’s stop, just a short walk from his house. Tommy exited the bus, followed by a handful of people he didn’t recognise.

The walk home took Tommy along a footpath, which led behind a long row of houses; the gardens to his right, a small pond to his left, hidden behind a sporadic line of trees. The path itself was bathed intermittently with the orange glow of the overhead streetlights. As he walked along the footpath, Tommy looked down the steep bank into the pond, and saw the wheels of an upturned shopping trolley protruding from the algae-covered surface of the water. On one hand, this kind of annoyed him, knowing the damage that this sort of pollution would be causing. But on the other hand, he knew that dumping a shopping trolley into a pond like this was *exactly* the sort of thing he himself might do.

He rolled his eyes at his own dumb thoughts, and continued on.

A man approached from the other end of the pathway, walking towards Tommy. He was little more than a silhouette, but as he passed under each successive streetlight, Tommy saw that he was wearing a black woollen hat and a dark jacket, and that his head was down, staring blankly at his feet.

As the man passed by, Tommy had to step slightly aside, to avoid walking directly into him. The man didn't even acknowledge his presence. *Fuckin' prick*, Tommy thought to himself, but decided against saying anything aloud. Who knew what kind of psycho this bloke might be?

Tommy continued on. Twice he looked back over his shoulder, just to see what that man was doing. As it so happened, he was doing nothing. He just continued walking in the opposite direction, before disappearing out of sight, onto the main road.

It was then that Tommy felt the presence of somebody else there with him.

Another man had emerged from one of the adjoining alleyways. He was wearing a balaclava, pulled down over his head, obscuring his face.

Tommy barely had any time to think before the point of some bladed instrument ripped into the side of his neck, a wave of pain tearing though his nerves like barbed wire. His breath caught in his lungs, a warmth growing, extending out from the wound inflicted to his throat.

Blood.

But this wasn't a fatal wound. It was just a scratch. A nasty scratch, for sure. But a scratch none the less.

Tommy saw what it was that had cut him; the man was holding a pair of garden shears, one thick, wooden handle in each hand. The man raised the shears once again.

Survival instincts kicking in, Tommy drove forward, desperately reaching for the man's throat, hoping that he might be able to get a tight enough grip, so that he could squeeze the life out of him. But the man simply stepped back. He raised the shears and snapped the blades shut.

The steel chomped through Tommy's fingers, cleanly slicing each one off, blood squirting from the remaining stumps.

Tommy screamed, grabbing at his wrist, hoping to stem the flow of blood from his ruined hand. But then his attacker drove the point of the shears upward, into his right armpit. Tommy felt the steel shred his flesh, and bite into his tendons, scraping against the bone. The man grunted as he twisted the handles and pulled the shears free.

A searing agony washed over Tommy, dropping him to his knees. He felt the man kick him then, a heavy boot slamming into his ribs. He was sure he felt the bones crack.

Rolling to his back, he looked up into the eyes of the masked man standing over him, only his eyes visible beyond the woollen façade, the orange of the streetlights causing them to glow inhumanly. The man held the shears over his head, the handles spread, the blades open wide like the gaping maw of a bloodthirsty shark.

"N-no…" muttered Tommy, barely able to form any words.

The man ignored him. He plunged the shears downward, driving the point of each blade into Tommy's respective eye sockets. The steel mulched the eyeballs with ease, and smashed through the flimsy orbital bone at the back, penetrating his skull, impaling his brain. Tommy heard the crack of the bone like the roar of thunder, hammering directly into his ear drums.

He wanted to scream. He wanted to call for help. But it was as if his body was no longer functioning correctly. He could taste blood oozing to the back of his throat, could feel it sliding over his lips.

The killer squeezed the handles of the shears together, the bone offering little in the way of resistance. The blades crunched through flesh and bone alike, until they slid comfortably together.

Tommy felt a sudden surge of pain, and then…

Nothing.

The killer left Tommy's corpse in the middle of the footpath, ready for the next passer-by to find, the garden shears still buried in his decimated face, standing upright, the handles reaching to the sky.

--- --- --- --- --- --- --- --- --- --- --- ---

Why do the killers in these movies always use household implements as their murder weapons? A kitchen knife. A pitchfork. A drill. A chainsaw. These are all items that people have access to, right at their very fingertips. Can we really feel safe if people are using these implements of death, while imagining the things they've seen in these movies? It would be so easy for somebody, just trimming their hedge, thinking about the movie they watched last night, and – BAM! – before they even realise what they've done, they've slashed somebody's throat with their garden shears. I cannot, in good conscience, stand by and let such atrocities take place.

Gary Smart, conservative MP and

campaigner against social liberalism

CHAPTER SIX:

DEAD KIDS

Caroline Thompson had lived on Wiltshire Avenue for the past forty-four years, and never in her life had she ever seen anything so horrific.

She and her husband Harold had moved into that little house in the same year they got married. They had both been twenty at the time. That was back in 1940 – shortly after the start of WWII. A year later, Harold was called up to the British army, and was sent off to fight in France. Less than a year after that, he was dead.

Caroline had been utterly heartbroken. She'd never re-married, never had any kids. And, for the past four decades, she'd lived alone in that house, with her memories of Harold her only company.

A few years ago, her younger sister Francesca had suggested that she ought to get herself a dog. It had to be lonely living alone. Caroline had insisted that she was fine, that she'd been alone for so many years that she'd simply gotten used to it. But Francesca wouldn't take no for an answer. As such, they had gone together to the rehoming centre, to find Caroline a new companion.

Barnaby was a west highland white terrier. Caroline had always imagined that she'd never feel love again, not after Harold had died. But she loved that little dog more than anything.

Every morning and every evening, Caroline walked Barnaby down the street, through the park – where he loved nothing more than chasing the squirrels – and back out onto the footpath beside the pond.

As they made their way out of the park, Caroline often stopped to look into the pond. She liked to watch the ducks there. Sometimes, if you looked closely, you could even see the frogspawn floating just beneath the surface.

But today, there was something else there.

Somebody had dumped a shopping trolley in there!

How could these kids do such a thing? Did they think it was funny? What were they trying to achieve. Kids nowadays had no respect. They didn't care about anything. It was all those horror movies they watched, and that… what did they call it? *Heavy Metal*, or something like that… It was all that rock music that was ruining their brains.

It was disgusting! Caroline would report this to the council as soon as she got home.

Barnaby was barking. Caroline had been so engrossed by the trolley in the pond, that she hadn't even noticed him disappearing out of the park. She followed the sound of his incessant yapping and found him out on the footpath.

His white fur was stained crimson.

There was a dead body lying on the path.

Caroline had never seen a dead body before, but she *knew* this boy was no longer amongst the living. Somebody had stabbed him in the face with a part of hedge trimmers. They been stabbed into his eye sockets. There was so much blood. It was everywhere, pooling on the path in a sticky scarlet puddle.

Caroline felt as if she were going to vomit.

She opened her mouth and emitted a blood curdling scream.

—

Helen's mind wandered through the entirety of her economics class. It was her first class of the day, and she simply couldn't focus. She wasn't sure if she was sick or not, but there was a horrible feeling writhing in the pit of her stomach. She felt as if her hands were shaking, like her muscles were weak. Perhaps she was coming down with something. Perhaps it was just the stress of everything that had happened, piling up on her.

At break time, she told Mark about how she'd felt. He suggested that maybe she just needed some sugar. She wasn't sure that was the answer, but still, when her offered her a chocolate digestive biscuit, she didn't refuse.

Much to her own surprise, it did make her feel somewhat better. She had three more, just to be on the safe side.

They had been sitting together on one of the picnic benches out in the courtyard. Lorraine, Anna, Chris and Ryan had all gone off campus to smoke. Although the college accepted that their students *could* smoke – and that they would if they so desired – it was still not allowed on the campus grounds. Ten minutes later, Helen was surprised to see Lorraine jogging across the field towards her. Lorraine *never* ran. She never jogged. As such, Helen immediately knew that something was wrong. "What's going on?" she asked, as Lorraine arrived at the bench, somewhat out of breath.

"You're never gonna fucking believe this!" said Lorraine, sucking in a deep lungful of air. She hunched over, supporting her weight on the bench. For a moment, Helen considered the fact that she might be about to collapse.

"What is it?" Helen asked. She could feel herself frowning. Her heart was babbling uncomfortably in her chest.

Lorraine shook her head, a solemn look on her face. Her cheeks were flushed bright red. "They found another body!"

A strange coldness flooded Helen's veins, like her blood had turned to icy slush. Her heart was racing now, the sickness in her stomach returning with a vengeance. This wasn't possible, surely not.

"What are you talking about?" said Mark, the look on his face clearly betraying the fact that he simply couldn't believe what he was being told.

But Helen believed it. She'd known this was coming. She'd felt it in her bones after Amy and Tina had been killed. She'd known that wasn't the end. Somehow, she knew that was just the beginning.

"They found another body!" Lorraine repeated. Anna, Chris and Ryan strolled up casually behind her. "They said he got stabbed in his eyes!"

The image turned Helen's stomach. How could somebody be so cruel?

"Are you fucking serious?" scoffed Mark, disgusted at the thought.

Lorraine nodded.

"She's not kidding," said Chris, hooking an arm around Lorraine's waist. "They think it was the same person who killed Amy and Tina."

Mark shrugged. "And what makes them think that?"

Chris shrugged his own shoulders in return.

"Who was it?" asked Helen, finally regaining her composure, having managed to once again stifle the sickening feeling in her gut.

"The killer?" said Chris.

"The victim," Helen confirmed.

"Some guy called Tom, apparently," Chris said. "Apparently he used to go to school here, but that was a few years back."

"They said an old lady found him," said Ryan, a smirk on his face. "They said he had scissors stuck in both of his eyes. Imagine that old lady's face!" He had to raise a hand to his mouth, to prevent himself laughing.

"It's not funny," said Helen. "Somebody's dead. And if it was the same killer, then that means we might actually be looking at a serial killer."

"Come on," said Chris, rolling his eyes. "I don't think it's that serious."

"What do you mean?" Helen's voice wavered. She could feel herself growing hysterical. "The killer's still out there. Any one of us could be next."

"Well let's just hope the police find whoever did it, huh?"

Helen's concentration only worsened as the day progressed. She had an English class after break, the duration of which she spent in some sort of a stupor, her mind flitting from one thought to the next, each one more horrifying as the last.

Was this really a serial killer?

Who was it?

Why were they doing this?

What did they want?

Who were they going to kill next?

What if they killed Lorraine or Anna?

What if they killed Mark?

What if they killed her*?*

She couldn't help but think about her mother. She'd been through so much over the years, Helen knew her mother was fragile. How was she going to react to the news that somebody else had been killed? She wasn't the type of person to say *'I told you so'*, but she would almost certainly let Helen know that she had been right all along. And there was no way for Helen to deny this fact; she *had been* right after all, the killer *was* still out there. There was no way she'd even contemplate letting Helen out of the house now. That was it. Helen would have to live her life in isolation, until the authorities caught whoever it was behind this.

Helen had a free period next. She made her way up to the library, so that she could read through one of her textbooks in peace. If it were the summertime, she'd have gone and sat out on the lawn, but it was far too cold for that now.

As she made her way to the top of the stairs and pulled open the library door, she paused momentarily at the sound of her own name.

Was somebody talking about her?

Helen tilted her head and listened intently. It took just a second for her to catch up on this thread of conversation.

Although she couldn't see who it was – they were hidden behind a row of bookshelves – she understood that they were indeed talking about her.

And they were talking about her mother.

"She's fucking crazy, that's what I heard," said one of the voices.

"She survived that massacre, like, twenty years ago, right?" said another voice.

"Yeah. Some maniac chopped her friends to pieces," said a third distinct voice.

"That's why you never see her mother leave the house."

"That's fucked up."

"Yeah, and that's why Helen's such a freak herself."

"Imagine having a parent who's completely insane."

"That's probably why her dad left too – he couldn't put up with that crazy bitch."

"Do you think she'd dangerous?"

"Maybe… I mean, it wouldn't surprise me if we found out that she's the one who killed Tina and Amy, and now this other kid."

Somebody laughed.

Helen could feel her heart breaking.

"Seriously? What are you talking about?"

"It's nearly Halloween – that's when it happened. It's nearly the anniversary."

"So?"

"So, that's what happens. Some ancient trauma gets dragged up, somebody snaps, and then they embark on a killing spree of their own. It happens in all the movies. Haven't you ever seen *Rosemary's Killer* or *Prom Night?*"

"The same thing happens in *Friday The 13th!*"

"Exactly!"

"And *you* think *she's* crazy…"

There was more laughter then. That was when Helen decided to leave. She turned and exited the library, deciding that she didn't even want to know who it was up there, talking about her mother.

She sprinted along the corridor, doing her best to ignore all the eyes staring at her. She pushed through the double doors and out into the fresh air, jumping down the stairs, and not stopping until she was in the middle of the lawn. That was when her legs gave out from under her. She dropped to her knees and began to cry.

She didn't even know *what* she was crying about. It wasn't nice hearing people speak ill of somebody you loved, sure. But that wasn't it. Helen already knew people talked about her mum that way. Even Helen herself couldn't really deny the fact that her mother was a little crazy. Perhaps it was the suggestion that her mother was responsible for the murders that had really upset her. No – that wasn't it either; that was just crazy talk. Surely nobody really believed her capable of that.

No. Helen knew what it was that had upset her. Those girls had mentioned her father. The idea that her mother may have driven him away with her apparent insanity was a terrible thing to think. That wasn't what had happened at all. Her father had had an affair. He'd left Helen's mother for some skinny blonde bimbo who worked in his office. They'd moved away, to the other end of the country, just about as far away as they could possibly get. Helen hadn't seen her dad in years. And the truth was, she didn't really care; she hated him for abandoning them the way he had.

But then another thought popped into Helen's mind, something all the more upsetting; what if it *was* her mother's insanity that had driven her father into the arms of another woman?

Fuck… Helen was starting to think like those girls now. Her mother wasn't even insane! Yes, she was cautious. There was a fear still brooding within her, which manifested itself as a deep concern for

Helen's well-being. But that was understandable, wasn't it? She'd been through hell. That didn't make her crazy.

But what if she was the killer?

What if she really had snapped…

No.

A hand landed on Helen's shoulder, scaring her half to death, snapping her out of her current train of thought. Helen gasped as she turned, and saw Kevin standing behind her, his eyebrows turned down in a look of concern. "Helen?" he asked, his voice soft. "Are you okay?"

Quickly, Helen sucked in a breath. She turned and pulled away. She pushed herself back up to her feet, and wiped her tears away on the back of her hand. "I'm fine," she said.

"Really? You don't look fine."

"Well, I am."

Kevin was still just as handsome as ever. He had rugged features and thick stubble, his black hair combed to one side, his brown eyes bright enough to pierce into your soul. But he was also a cheat. One lunch time, Helen had gone with Lorraine and Anna to smoke a cigarette just outside the back gate of the college. They had found Kevin there, with his tongue down Melanie Harper's throat, and his hands on her tits.

Kevin had been so apologetic, for a moment Helen had considered that perhaps she ought to forgive him. But Lorraine had convinced her that he was only sorry that he'd been caught, and that once a cheat, always a cheat. That had made perfect sense to Helen. She didn't ever want to see him again.

But there was no getting away from the fact that they both attended the same college. It was inevitable that their paths would sometimes cross. But whenever he tried to talk to her, she'd simply turn her back and ignore him.

But, deep down, there was something inside her that was glad to be looking upon a friendly face at that very moment.

She shook the thought from her head.

"You seem upset," Kevin continued. "What's wrong?"

Helen sighed. "I don't know. Nothing. Everything, maybe. I think it's all just gotten too much for me. First Amy and Tina, and now this… God – it's all completely fucked."

Kevin smirked, offering just the hint of a laugh. "Yeah. I know what you mean."

Helen offered her own smile in return.

"Hey, dickhead," said a voice from somewhere behind Kevin.

Helen tilted her head to look past Kevin, and saw Lorraine marching towards them.

"What the fuck do you think you're doin', huh?" Lorraine continued. "I thought I told you to leave Helen alone."

"She's upset," said Kevin, rolling his eyes, "she seemed like she needed help."

"Yeah, well – she doesn't need help from *you*." Lorraine hooked her arm around Helen's own, and began to drag her back towards the college.

"I'll see you later," Kevin called to Helen, his voice already beginning to fade.

Helen looked back to Kevin out the corner of her eye. She didn't respond.

Later, after her final class, Helen met up with Lorraine, Anna, Mark, Chris and Ryan once again. "Are you okay?" asked Mark, rubbing her shoulder. "I heard you were crying earlier. Is everything alright?"

Helen nodded. "I'm fine," she confirmed. "I just got a little overwhelmed, I think."

"That's understandable." He nodded sympathetically.

"Yeah, well," said Anna, her eyebrows raised. "At least we've got the Halloween party coming up, to take our minds off things."

Helen had forgotten about the annual Halloween party. Ever since the massacre, the town had no longer thrown its own annual party. As such, over the years the town's kids had improvised, throwing their own party in the old, abandoned slaughterhouse, on the outskirts of town. But Helen wasn't in the mood for a party, not now, not this year. "Surely the party will be cancelled this year," she said. "Wouldn't it be a bit disrespectful?"

"Yeah," said Mark. "And with a killer on the loose, wouldn't a party be like a red flag to a bull, begging them to come and kill a bunch of people?"

"Hey, that reminds me," said Ryan, before anybody had the opportunity to respond. "Before we head home, I need to drop into the video shop, to return this tape." He lifted his bag, indicating that the tape to which he was referring was inside.

"Oh, yeah," said Chris. "Did you watch it? Was it any good?"

Ryan nodded his head. "Yeah, it was pretty brutal! It's a bit weird, but when they guy finally goes crazy and starts killing everybody, it gets pretty nasty. I can understand why they'd try to ban it."

Helen couldn't remember what film it was that Ryan had borrowed. She expected that it didn't really matter; as far as she was concerned, all horror movies were the same. She assumed the same could only be said for the 'video nasties.'

"Anyway," Ryan continued. "I wanna see if he's got a film called *Contamination*. It looks pretty sick."

"Yeah, alright," said Lorraine. "Let's just get going then, shall we."

"Alright."

As they crossed the college grounds, Anna linked arms with Helen. "The party," she said, "you *are* coming, right?"

Helen sighed. "I don't know."

Anna smiled. "Yeah, you're coming!"

Helen rolled her eyes and laughed.

The six of them left the college grounds and followed the road, cutting through the alley, and into the shopping centre. Immediately, they stopped. A crowd had amassed outside of Video Magic. There must've been thirty or forty people there. There were a number of police officers there, their arms stretched wide, holding the crowd back. A man with a camera mounted on his shoulder pushed through the cluster of people, towards the front of the shop.

"What the fuck is going on?" muttered Chris.

"I have no idea…" Ryan replied.

Helen knew what had happened – they'd found another body. Russ. He was dead. Somebody had killed him.

But then there was a commotion from inside, and Russ was led out of the shop – alive and well, albeit with his hands pinned behind his back by the two police officers who were marching him out of the shop.

The cameraman pushed in close, the lens of his camera nearly pressing against Russ' face.

"I haven't done anything!" shouted Russ. "This is fucking crazy! You can't arrest me for this shit!"

Another officer exited the shop, carrying a box which Helen recognised to be the one from which Russ had pulled his collection of video nasties. The officer held the box low, so that another man – this one dressed in a brown suit, with a black pinstripe tie – could look inside. He then turned to Russ, holding up a handful of video tapes for all to see. "Oh, really?" said the man. "What's this then?"

"They're just films, for fuck's sake! That doesn't mean I killed anybody!"

Killed anybody? Had Russ been accused of the murders?

It was then that Helen recognised the man in the suit. She'd seen him before, on TV. It was that politician – Gary Smart, the one who had been pushing to ban the video nasties. The police officers shoved the crowd backwards, clearing a pathway for Russ to be escorted to the waiting car.

“We all know what effect these movies have on young, impressionable minds,” said Gary. “With your existing criminal record, I think it’s easily imaginable that you might’ve been adversely affected by this filth!”

Helen frowned. She looked to Ryan. “Criminal record?” she asked, hoping he might know what Russ had done.

Ryan shook his head. “He got busted for drugs once,” he said. “That’s about it.”

“I’m not some sort of psychopath!” yelled Russ, as the police officers manhandled him into the car, shoving his head down and pushing him back. “I didn’t do anything!”

The car was gone then, and the crowd began to disperse.

The remaining police officers began to file into the video shop. “Check everything,” said the commanding officer. “Leave no stone unturned. There has to be some kind of evidence in there.”

The cameraman remained, his focus now on Gary Smart. Helen hadn’t noticed before, but there was a journalist amongst the crowd. He pushed in close to Gary, a microphone held up to his face. “Mr. Smart! What is it you believe has happened here?” the journalist asked.

Gary turned. He looked directly into the lens of the camera. “Evil has come to this town,” said the politician, all very dramatic. “And it has come in the guise of the video nasties. This young man’s mind has been corrupted by the violent imagery he has been viewing.”

“So, you believe that he is responsible for the killing of the boy last night, and of the two girls the night before?”

“I believe it is entirely possible, yes. This is a troubled young man; these videos can only have served to make him even more so. They destroy the mind, leading people to commit acts which they normally never would do. And this could happen in any town next. Video rental stores need to be searched, in every corner of our country. This is the only way we can hope to keep our children safe!”

“But, are you certain this is the murderer? Is the killer off the streets?”

"Even if this boy isn't the killer, then the killer himself will soon be caught. There is no doubt in my mind that this monster has been influenced by the video nasties. The person we have just arrested will know who the killer is. He'll know everybody who has ever rented these films before. If he isn't directly responsible, then he will most certainly be able to assist us."

The journalist nodded. "MP Gary Smart, thank you."

"Thank you." Gary Smart then disappeared into the video shop.

The journalist turned back to face the camera. "Are the streets now safe? Has a killer been locked up? And are violent horror movies really to blame? Only time will tell."

Helen was shocked. She couldn't quite believe what she'd just seen. "Is it possible that Russ did it?" she asked the others.

"No way," said Ryan, shaking his head dismissively. "I've known him for years. He's no psycho."

"That politician seemed pretty sure he did it," said Anna.

"Yeah, well – that politician doesn't know what he's talking about."

"How can you be so sure?"

"Trust me," said Ryan. "I'm sure."

Helen wasn't so sure. Was it possible that these movies really could turn people into psychopaths? A number of seemingly intelligent people seemed to think this was the case. But none of that really made sense. She knew people who watched these films – Ryan and Chris, for starters. Even Lorraine had seen some of them. None of them had turned psychotic. But she didn't know Russ like she knew them; maybe he *was* the killer.

She could only hope that he was. Not that she wanted it to be him, but at least then she'd know that the killer was behind bars. Maybe then they could all sleep soundly at night.

"One thing I do know," said Ryan. "Is that he ain't gonna be wanting this tape back in a hurry, is he?"

--- --- --- --- --- --- --- --- --- --- --- ---

We all know that crime rates are currently through the roof. The statistics prove this to be the case. But we don't need statics to show us this; we can simply look out of our windows, or step out of our front doors, and see society crumbling before our very eyes. There is violence on every street corner. And why is this the case? What's changed over the past decade, to have caused such a significant rise? I'll tell you, shall I? The media has changed. Kids are watching more TV. They're reading violent comic books. And then there's the video nasties. All of these things have seen a sharp rise over the past few years, in direct conjunction with this steep rise in crime. Is this a coincidence? I think not.

Margret Whitehead, conservative activist and author of

'Violence On Video: The End Of Morality?'

Chapter Seven:

Visiting Hours

"This is fucking insane," said Russ, shaking his head. "I didn't do anything."

"I'll ask you once again to refrain from using such vulgar language," said the investigating officer, seated on the opposite side of the table. This man was broad shouldered, with wavy brown hair, and a thick moustache. He seemed to constantly be smoking cigarettes; as soon as one was finished and extinguished in the flimsy foil ashtray, another was immediately ignited. He had introduced himself as Detective Chief Inspector Hanbury. "Surely you know you shouldn't use such language in the presence of a lady?"

Beside him, a female officer was seated. Her blonde hair was wild and frizzy, barely controlled by the excessive amounts of hairspray she'd undoubtedly used in an attempt to tame it. She wore a white blouse with a large collar, and a grey blazer with thick padding in the shoulders. She too was smoking a cigarette, her arms folded, holding it delicately to the side of her head. Her name was Detective Inspector Wells.

"And besides," said DCI Hanbury, stamping out another cigarette butt. "Your aggressive tone doesn't do you any favours in convincing us that you're not some sort of a serial killer."

Russ raised his eyebrows. "This is bullshit."

Hanbury shook his head. "You're not helping yourself." He lit up another smoke.

"Anyway," said DI Wells, sitting forward in her chair, nonchalantly flipping through the stack of papers that she had pulled from a cardboard file. "Let me ask you again; when do you think you decided to start killing people? Was it a conscious decision, or…"

"I didn't kill anyone," Russ sighed.

"Well, our psychoanalysts seem to think that you match the profile perfectly. A young, white, male. Heavy use of marijuana. A fan of disturbing horror films. Tell me, do you get a kick out of hurting people?"

Russ shook his head, almost in disbelief. "I don't get it," he said, exasperated. "Is this some kind of joke? Is somebody playing a prank on me? Is this supposed to be funny?"

"Do you think murder is funny?"

Russ slumped back in his chair, his hands behind his head. "Oh. My. God. This is fucking ridiculous."

"Just answer the question, please. Do you find murder funny?"

"No. I don't."

"But you enjoy so-called *slasher* movies, right?"

"I…" Russ considered his answer, trying to sidestep this obvious attempt at entrapment. He shrugged his shoulders. "Lots of people enjoy slasher films, myself being one of them. That doesn't make me a murderer."

"No, committing murder makes you a murderer," said Hanbury, puffing away at his cigarette. "So, *why* did you kill those girls? Did you get some sort of sexual pleasure from it?"

Russ scoffed a laugh, couldn't stop himself.

"Do you think this is funny? Three people are dead. There could be more, so far as we know. And all signs point towards you as being their killer. Did you kill them?"

Russ sat forward in his chair. "For the five-thousandth time – no, I didn't kill them. Nor did I kill anybody. I *knew* Tommy Stone. He was a friend of mine."

Wells nodded, scribbling notes in her pad.

"Did you ever sell drugs to Tom Stone?" asked Hanbury.

Russ shrugged his shoulders. "Yeah, maybe," he said, knowing there was little point in lying about it, since they already had his criminal record on hand. He sold a bit of weed to a few acquaintances. So what? It was hardly the crime of the century, was it? He'd been given a six-month suspended sentence last year, for possession with an intent to supply. Big deal. That didn't make him a psychopath, did it?

"Did he owe you money?" the detective asked.

Fuck me, thought Russ. They were trying really hard to pin this on him. What frustrated him most about it all wasn't the fact that they had him locked up in there, it was that they weren't out there searching for the real killer. "No. He didn't."

"Are you sure? Are you sure you didn't kill him 'cause he didn't pay his debt?"

"What if I did?" said Russ, already knowing that engaging in this conversation was probably a stupid thing to do. "If that was my motive for killing him, then why did I kill those two girls?"

Hanbury sat back in his seat, eyebrows raised, nodding his head as if he were almost impressed. "So, we're talking about *motives* now," he said, almost mockingly.

Wells smiled, as if this were somehow amusing to her.

Russ was growing more furious by the second. He could feel his cheeks growing warm, no doubt turning them a blotchy shade of red. Tears threatened to spill from his heavy eyelids. He was going to jail. They were going to lock him up and throw away the key. All for something *he didn't do*. And then, even as the killings continued, even as he continued to protest his innocence, they'd still keep him locked up, claiming that they were certain he was responsible for the first murders, and that these new killings were the work of some other killer, and that this was an entirely unrelated incident. His life was over; he'd might as well just kill himself.

"Let's talk about the 'video nasties'," said Hanbury, using his fingers to make air quotes around the phrase. "We found a large collection of prohibited films in your shop. They belong to you, yes?"

Russ sighed once more, slumping back in his seat, exhausted. "Yes."

"And you continued to rent them out to the public?"

"No. Only my friends."

"Are you aware that still counts as distribution, so that's still illegal?"

Russ shrugged his shoulders. "I guess."

"And you don't care about the damage that they might be doing to people?"

"They aren't doing any damage to people. Only a fucking idiot would believe that."

Hanbury raised his eyebrows. "Is that so? Tell me, when did you get your qualification in psychology? Are you a doctor? Or a scientist, perhaps?"

Russ rolled his eyes, looked away. "No."

"No?" smirked Hanbury. "Then how do you know they aren't causing severe psychological damage to those who view them? It seems quite clear to me that they've had a negative effect on you. They've turned you into a serial killer!"

Russ gritted his teeth. "I didn't kill anyone!" he said, lurching forward, his chest and arms crashing into the table before him. It hurt, but he didn't really care.

Hanbury extinguished his cigarette and sat back in his chair. He looked to Wells, who then finished her own cigarette, and stubbed it out too. Hanbury turned his gaze back to Russ. "Yeah," he said, knowingly. "I think they're gonna lock you up for a very long time."

The smug bastard looked incredibly pleased with himself.

The door to the interview room opened, and a younger officer entered the room. "Can I have a moment?" he asked the two detectives.

"Sure," said Hanbury. "I think we're nearly done here anyway." He and Wells then stood from their respective seats and followed the young officer out of the room.

Russ was only alone for a few moments, but that was enough time for his brain to burn through a million different scenarios. Not one of them was good. He imagined himself in a prison cell. He imagined himself being beaten to a pulp by his follow inmate. He imagines himself growing old behind bars, never seeing his family again, never having a family of his own. He imagined tying a noose around his own neck.

The door to the interview room opened once again, and DCI Hanbury and DI Wells re-entered. Hanbury stood by the door, his arms folded across his chest, his face crumpled up into a ferocious scowl. He looked entirely pissed off. It was Wells who approached the table. "Well," she said, bending over, propping her weight up on her extended arms. "It looks as if we're letting you go."

This surprised Russ. It was just about the last thing he'd expected. "What? Really?"

"Yes. It seems we don't have enough evidence to nail you with the murders."

"Of course you don't," said Russ, standing from his seat. "That's 'cause I didn't do it."

"Yeah, well… we're still not sure about that. But until we get some more evidence, then I guess you're free to go."

Russ stepped out from behind the table and made his way towards the door. "What about the tapes?" he asked, immediately regretting the question, knowing that he shouldn't have asked it. Perhaps they might've forgotten about them.

"We'll be back to see you about them at a later date. It's up to the CPS if they want to press charges, and they haven't made a decision just yet."

Russ nodded, and headed for the door. As he passed, Hanbury took a firm grip of his arm, stopping him in his tracks. "Try not kill anybody, okay?"

"Yeah," said Russ. "I'll try to control myself."

DCI Hanbury was seething, steam on the verge of venting from his ears, and, in that very moment, nothing could've made Russ happier.

—

The pigs had done a real number on the shop. It was as if a bomb had gone off, or as if a tornado had ripped through the building, tearing every single tape off of its respective shelf. Plastic cases laid strewn about the floor, wide open, sleeves torn, their respective tapes scattered. The display stand by the door – where Russ put the new releases – had been knocked over. As it had fallen, it had seemingly caught on the *Mad Max* poster that hung in the window, tearing it down.

Russ wanted to cry. The place was destroyed. It would take him days – if not weeks – to get everything back in order. He hadn't expected to find it like this. As he'd pulled away the police tape that spanned the door, and pushed his way inside, he'd expected to find the place pretty much how he'd left it. That was far from the case.

A flaming anger boiled his piss. Why would they have done this? Was any of it necessary? What were they hoping to achieve? The shop was insured of course, but he imagined the insurance company wouldn't be so keen to pay for these damages. They'd have considered them preventable, like it was somehow Russ' fault this had happened, like it was his fault that he'd been arrested for a murder he didn't commit.

He wondered if he might be able to claim compensation from the police force.

Highly unlikely. Besides, it wasn't worth drawing any more unwanted attention to himself. He'd just have to try and salvage everything he could. Perhaps it wouldn't be so bad. Perhaps it *looked* worse than it really was.

Behind the counter, all the tapes he kept stored there had been opened up and dumped into bin liners. And it wasn't just the horror films they had targeted; it was everything. Comedy. Action. Family.

Had they really thought he might've been hiding a copy of *Faces Of Death* in the case for *Fantasia*? Or maybe *SS Experiment Camp* in the case for *Star Trek: The Motion Picture*? That would be a dumb move, even for Russ. What if he forgot, and some kid rented *Lady And The Tramp*, only to find themselves watching Bob Belling rape a goat in *Island Of Death*? As funny as that might've been, he'd have certainly found himself knee-deep in dog shit.

All of his rental books were gone. There was no way for him to know who had borrowed what now. There was no way for him to know what or when any given tape was due back. He'd have to take stock of all of his inventory. Anything that was missing, he'd just have to assume he was never going to get back.

This whole fucking situation was fucked!

Russ swung his foot and kicked through a pile of tapes, then instantly regretted it. He'd heard the plastic crack; that could've been a few hundred pounds worth of cassette he'd just destroyed.

Fuck it. Just add it to the total.

He squatted down and scooped up a pile of sleeveless tapes. The first tape on top of the pile was Betamax copy of *Return Of The Jedi*. Russ scanned the cases that surrounded him. Surely the correct case couldn't have gone far. Low and behold – there it was. Russ returned the cassette to the case.

One down, nine-hundred and ninety-nine more to go.

That was being optimistic.

Russ needed something to calm his nerves. Thankfully, he knew just the thing. As the police had let him go, he felt certain they hadn't found his secret stash of weed. He looked out through the front window of the shop, to see that the sun was now setting, and that there was nobody hanging around outside watching him.

He made his way across the shop and into the back room, where the small toilet was situated. There, he lifted the lid from the cistern and retrieved a kilogram bag of weed from inside. The bag itself was sealed tight, but it had then been wrapped in cling film and taped around a half-dozen times, to ensure that it was watertight. Thankfully, the pigs had been too focused on looking for illegal video tapes – or evidence of murder – so they hadn't bothered looking for his drugs. Had they have found them; he'd surely have been looking at a few years locked away.

Thank God for small mercies.

Russ peeled open the edge of the bag, tugging the corner of the film until it came away from the tape. He lifted the package to his nose and sniffed. The contents smelled glorious.

He snapped a cigarette and rolled it between his fingers, squeezing out the tobacco and transposing it into the open rolling paper he'd rested on his knee. He then pinched a bud of marijuana from the packet, and crumbled it in. He rolled the joint, licked along the length, and sealed it. He placed it between his lips and ignited the end, drawing in the sweet smoke until his lungs were filled to capacity. He held it there for a moment, then exhaled, a great cloud of white smoke filling the room.

A calming sensation filled his body, starting as a tingle in his fingertips, then dancing its way along his arms and filling his chest.

His mellow was then immediately struck dead by the sound of the shop door opening.

Fuck! thought Russ. It had to be the police. They'd come for him. He was screwed now. The stubbed the spliff out on the side of the porcelain toilet bowl, then dropped the remains into the toilet and flushed.

"If you hadn't noticed," he said, as he stepped out of the back room. "We're closed."

There was nobody there.

Perhaps whoever it was had planned to rob the place. They'd thought it was empty, thought they'd help themselves to whatever it was they could find. Then maybe when they'd realised Russ was actually there, they'd fled.

Or maybe it was just the wind. It had happened before. On more than one occasion, Russ had gone to speak to a customer, only to find that there was nobody there, and that a gust had simply rattled the door.

"Hello?" said Russ, just to be sure he wasn't going crazy. He was already feeling a little stoned, the weed having already started to take effect.

There was no reply.

He stepped further out into the shop, assuming that he'd at least see *something*. The door was firmly closed, the battered and broken tapes remained undisturbed in their disordered piles. Whoever it was who had tried to enter the shop – if it even *was* a person at all – was no longer present.

No.

They were still there, standing to Russ' left. He hadn't seen them hidden there in the shadow, as they were dressed all in black. Even their head was covered, a black balaclava pulled down over their face. It wasn't until he saw the purple light of the setting sun glint from the blade of their exposed razor that he noticed them there.

"What the fuck?" Russ bellowed, turning, almost losing his footing as his feet scattered cassettes.

A flash of light indicated that the blade was now rushing towards him. Without warning, his man – whoever the fuck it was – he swiped at Russ with the razor. Russ didn't even see it coming. The sharpened steel sliced through the flesh of his cheek with absolute ease, parting the meat like a chicken breast. A surge of warmth pulsed from Russ' face, followed by agonising pain. He could feel the blood rushing from the wound, soaking into his t-shirt.

Russ gasped. He opened his mouth wide, wanting to scream, but finding he couldn't, the function of his lungs seemingly having given out.

The man in black slashed towards him again.

Russ raised his hands, hoping to defend himself.

The blade of the razor whipped through the meat of his fingers as if they weren't even there. The steel bounced from each of the bones, plasma spraying from the deep lacerations, and pooling in his palm.

Russ clamped his hands together, hoping to stem the flow of blood. But this only served to leave him wide open, unable to fight back.

The killer swung once more. This time, the savage stainless sliced through Russ' throat, chewing through his larynx, and opening up his carotid artery.

Russ watched, wide eyed, as his blood evacuated his body, long jets of crimson, spraying from the hole in his neck like a red ribbon. It coated the counter, splattering the walls. Russ stumbled forward, his hands clawing at his throat, his attempts to close the wound an exercise in futility. He dropped to his knees and fell face first into a pile of broken VHS tapes.

As the life slipped out of him, his vision growing fuzzy, Russ watched his blood spraying over the cassettes scattered before him.

And the last thought that ran through his mind, was that those tapes were now ruined.

--- --- --- --- --- --- --- --- --- --- --- ---

What concerns me more is the fact that these films clearly know they have something to hide. I would bet my last penny that most people have never heard of Carnage *or* Twitch Of The Death Nerve, *but these are both titles that the movie* Blood Bath *was released under – why change the title, unless you don't want people to know that this movie you are releasing is actually the same grotesquely violent slasher that was banned just last week? And there's more –* Don't Open The Window, Make Them Die Slowly, Toxic Zombies, Night School, The Dorm That Dripped Blood… *All films they have tried to release on more than one occasion. Why try to trick the public in such a way? Isn't this the purest definition of evil?*

Gary Smart, conservative MP and

campaigner against social liberalism

CHAPTER EIGHT:

ABSURD

Wendy just couldn't understand why Helen – her own daughter, her own flesh and blood – was being this way. Another boy had been killed; Wendy had heard about it from Sally once again, an endless fountain of gossip. Only this wasn't gossip. This was a serious matter. There was a killer on the loose, for God's sake! Teenagers were being murdered! It was entirely possible that Helen could be next. There was no way Wendy was going to let that happen.

"They've arrested somebody, Mom!" Helen protested. "They've got him locked up down at the police station. I saw them take him away!"

"And what if they've got the wrong person?" Wendy countered. "The killer might still be out there!"

"So what if he is!" Helen yelled, her voice cracking, tears filling her eyes. "You can't stop me from living my life! I can take care of myself!"

Wendy hated seeing Helen upset like this. She'd seen it far too many times over the years. They argued often, normally brought on by what Helen would call Wendy's 'irrational fears.' But there was nothing *irrational* about it. Once upon a time, she herself had nearly been a victim. And despite the fact that she had survived, and that she herself had put a stop to that maniac, that night still haunted her. Why couldn't Helen see that she was just trying to protect her from the same fate?

"I know you can, Helen!" Wendy said, her own voice raised. "Under any *normal* circumstances, I know that would be the case. But these *aren't* normal circumstances!"

"So… what?" argued Helen. "I'm supposed to just lock myself away in my bedroom, never go out again?"

"Yes! That's exactly what you need to do! Just until the killer is caught."

"They *have* caught him! I just told you that!"

"And *I'm* telling *you*, *I* don't trust them to have gotten the right guy!"

Helen had told Wendy that she was going out, that she intended to go around to Anna's house. When Wendy had asked why, Helen had insisted that they would just be hanging out, and that they'd maybe watch a movie or something. The thought of Helen alone in that house with only her friend for company, made Wendy conjure an image of those two girls in her mind – the two girls who had been brutally murdered just a few short nights ago. And now there was this boy – stabbed to death with garden shears – meaning that this really *was* a serial killer, and that this was almost certainly just the beginning.

"This is bullshit!" screamed Helen. "You can't stop me from going out."

"Oh yes I can, young lady! I'm your mother!"

"So, what are you going to do? Lock me in my bedroom?"

"If that's what it takes, yes! Under no circumstances are you to leave this house!"

Helen scoffed, rolling her eyes. "Oh, go to hell!" She stormed off then, her feet pounding the floor as she hurried along to the front door, damn-near pulling it off its hinges as she stormed out of the house.

"You get back here this instant!" Wendy shouted, before she'd even realised that Helen had gone. Almost immediately, panic began to gnaw at Wendy's bones. Helen had gone… She'd left the house… She was in serious danger out there… Why would she do that? Why wouldn't she listen to her mother?

"Helen?" Wendy whimpered, tears now rolling down her cheeks. Why did everything have to turn into an argument? She shouldn't have spoken to her like that. She'd driven Helen away. And now, she might've just put her in danger. "Helen…"

—

For a brief moment, Helen hated her mother.

It took just a second for that feeling to dissipate, however, as she realised that her mother had only wanted what was best for her. Helen understood that her mother cared about her. She'd been around Helen's age when George Milton had attacked her and her friends, leaving her as the only survivor. She could probably see a lot of herself in Helen. But then, why couldn't she see her as a survivor? She had survived that massacre all those years ago. She was strong and brave and powerful. So why didn't she *feel* that way?

The sun had set now, the sky having turned a deep shade of purple, a blanket of shadow smothering the earth.

Helen had been heading towards Anna's house, intending to continue with her evening as planned. But something inside was nagging at her, telling her that she ought to go home, not because of the potential danger she may have been in, but so that she could apologise to her mother. She was probably scared, fearing for her daughter's life. She shouldn't have been; but Helen knew that she would.

Still, Helen was tense. She needed to calm down before she went back home. If she walked into the house so tightly wound, there was every chance she might explode, and then a whole other argument would likely erupt. She and her mother would be at each other's throats once again.

She decided to just take some time to walk around the block, to clear her mind. She could go back in twenty minutes or so, and then maybe she and her mother could try and have a reasonable conversation.

The first thought that crossed Helen's mind was that of whether or not she and her friends were actually safe now. The police had arrested Russ. She'd tried to convince her mother that this fact alone made her safe. She'd said not, and, truth be told, Helen didn't believe it either. She didn't know Russ all too well, but she didn't think that he was the sort of person to go around killing people. And this idea that his watching video nasties might've been the cause… That was simply preposterous.

But if it *wasn't* Russ, then who? If it wasn't Russ, then that meant her mother was right; the killer was still on the loose. And if the killer was still free to roam the streets, then anybody could've been next.

Even Helen herself might be a victim.

Helen felt her heart flutter nervously, a pinch in her gut trying to convince her that leaving the house was a mistake, and that she should've listened to her mother. She looked back over her shoulder, suddenly feeling an awkward sensation, like somebody was watching her.

Somebody *was* there, a hundred yards or so away. They were just standing there, motionless. From this distance, it was impossible to tell in which direction they were looking. But Helen could sense their eyes on her, penetrating her, as if they were searching for her soul.

Helen didn't stop. She continued walking, increasing her pace, not wanting to be within sight of that man – she was *sure* it was a man; his silhouette betrayed the fact – for any longer than was entirely necessary. As she neared the street corner, she looked back once again to see that the man was now gone.

Gone.

Gone where?

Shit. She needed to get out of there. She needed to get home. Was it the killer who had been watching her? It wasn't likely, but still the thought terrified her.

Around the corner, Helen broke into a light jog, her heartrate now through the roof, adrenaline burning to the extremities of her body. She checked her surroundings, finding that she was on Turner Lane – a few streets up from her own home. There was shortcut just ahead, one that she'd taken a million times before. An alley led between two of the houses; a pathway to access the rear gardens. A row of trees separated this pathway from a second pathway, running along the back of the houses in the next street along. That was where she needed to go.

Helen cut into the alley, checking over her shoulder to make sure that nobody had followed her. If they had – and if they had bad intentions for her – there would be no possibility of her escaping now, not unless she could outrun them and make it through the trees and out onto the adjoining street.

But there was nobody behind her. Whoever that man was, he hadn't followed her.

Still, anxiety shook Helen's core. She just wanted to get home. At the backs of the houses, there was gap between two of the trees; a pathway carved by the hundreds of youths who had used this shortcut over the past few decades. Helen pushed through, knocking the branches aside so that they wouldn't catch in her hair. This green scar that separated the two alleys was just a few metres wide. It took Helen just a few seconds to navigate her way out onto the other side.

This side of the trees was like a mirror image of the alleyway she'd just left. To her right, a few houses down, would be the gap between the two houses, where she could make her way back out onto the road.

She turned, and headed in that direction.

Down the alley, and Helen froze in place.

There was a man standing before her, a silhouette against the moonlight that penetrated the alleyway, his frame filling the gap, as if his shoulders stretched from one house to the next, as if it might even be too tight for him to fit.

But then, all of a sudden, he was moving, lurching soundlessly towards her.

Helen screamed. She turned and ran. She hoped to God that somebody might have just heard her screams, and that they might call the police. Perhaps this possibility alone might be enough to stop the man from chasing her. If he was just trying to scare her, then the possibility of going to jail might be enough to stop his pursuit.

But when Helen looked back, he was still there, gaining on her now. He was too close; she'd never make the gap in the trees. She turned, her hands raised. "Please," she begged. "Stop!" Her heel caught on the edge of a mis-aligned slab, no doubt pushed out of place by the thick tree roots growing just below the surface. Her ankle twisted and Helen fell to the ground with a heavy thud, the shock sending a jolt of pain up her spine.

She looked up at the man, now able to get a clearer look at him. He was wearing a mask; a black balaclava, tightly wrapped around his skull. He wore a black jacket, and black trousers, and black boots, and black gloves, all of which made him almost invisible in the darkness. In his right hand he held a knife, a dark smear of grime on the blade.

Blood.

Helen was crying now, warm tears rolling down her flushed cheeks. "Why are you doing this?" she whimpered, about the best she could manage.

The man, breathing heavy, towered over her. He almost looked like a mountain, his frame blocking out the moonlight, bathing Helen in shadow. But he remained silent, only his raspy breaths emanating from his open mouth.

"Please," Helen sniffled, wishing that she were a braver person, knowing that her tears would probably only add to this maniac's excitement. She wanted to scream again – please God, let somebody have heard her! – but she knew this would only spur the man into killing her sooner. "What did I ever do to you? Please… don't kill me."

The masked man lifted the knife, his arm outstretched, the point of the blade aimed directly at Helen. He held it there for a moment, then lowered it, seemingly deciding against killing her.

But then he dropped to his knees, driving the blade downward, towards Helen's exposed neck.

Helen closed her eyes and held her breath, waiting for the inevitable sting of steel slicing through her flesh.

But it never came.

She opened her eyes and found that the man was now crouching over her, the blade of his knife hovering just a few millimetres away from her throat. He was playing with her. Toying with her, like a cat would a mouse. He wanted her to feel terror.

His plan had worked; Helen was petrified. She forced herself to breathe, each breath coming short and racked, her lungs rattling in her chest, like those of an eighty-year-old asthmatic. She looked up into the eyes of the man now perched upon her, looking down upon her. They were eyes she seemed to recognise.

Not that it mattered right now. What mattered now was her own survival.

She reached out with her right hand, scraping her fingers through the dirt that made up the ground beside the path. There, her hand fell upon a thick branch. For a moment, she considered if it might actually just be the exposed root of a tree. But it felt loose. And it felt heavy. She wrapped her palm around it and swung.

The man groaned as the heavy hunk of wood cracked into the side of his head, knocking him off balance. Helen kicked out, sending him rolling to the side, freeing her from his grasp. She scrambled up to her feet and ran.

But she could hear the man behind her, already up to his feet, already giving chase.

She needed to escape the alley. This psychopath wouldn't kill her out in the open, would he? Not right there, in the middle of the street, where hundreds of eyes might be upon him. Surely not. Helen was counting on it. She turned the corner and pushed her way along the gap between the two houses, her pursuer less than a few feet behind her.

And then she was out onto the street, rows of houses on either side, the lights on, but their curtains drawn. She screamed once again, hoping to draw attention.

The man was still there, right behind her. He'd followed her out of the alley.

Helen spun around, the branch still tightly held within her grasp. She swung it once again, this time taking aim for the knife. The branch slammed into the man's wrist, knocking the knife from his grip.

But that wasn't enough to stop him. He grabbed Helen, and used his own legs to trip her, send her sprawling to the ground, the back of her head bouncing from the tarmac, an agonising shockwave bursting outward from the point of impact.

The man was on her then, straddling her, his hands wrapped around her throat, squeezing. Helen felt her brain beginning to go numb as the blood supply was cut off. Her lungs burned as they tried desperately to suck in air.

Behind the mask, the man's teeth were gritted. He was snarling like a dog, as he choked the life out of Helen.

Out the corner of her eye, off to her right, Helen saw something on the ground. The cool blue of the moonlight danced from the grubby blade of the man's knife. She knew that it was within reach. Her hand sprang out, her fingers wrapped around the handle. She then drove the blade of the knife into the side of the man's chest.

Immediately, his grip loosened. Helen could feel the warmth of his blood oozing out over her hands, soaking into her sweatshirt, sticky against her skin.

With a panicked look in his eyes, the man removed his hand from Helen's neck. He sat up. As he did so, the blade slid out from between his ribs, causing more blood to gush forth.

But that wasn't enough for Helen. She rolled the knife over in her hand, then stabbed it directly into the man's chest, aiming for his heart. The amount of blood that immediately flowed from the wound told her that she might've just been successful in finding her target.

The man rolled off of Helen, onto his back. His breathing had already slowed, each breath laboured now, requiring extreme effort just to force his lungs to function.

Helen clambered up to her knees. She reached for the man's balaclava and lifted it from his face.

Immediately, her hands clasped over her mouth.

It was Mark.

What the fuck?

"M-Mark?" Helen stammered, unable to believe what she was seeing right before her very eyes. "Wh-what the fuck is going on? Why were you trying to kill me?"

Mark smiled. He sputtered a laugh, causing blood to spray from his lips. "I wasn't trying to kill you," he said. "I just wanted to scare you."

Helen shook her head, not understanding. "What? Is this just some sort of fucked up joke? Why would you do that?"

"Fear is powerful."

Still none the wiser, Helen suddenly thought of a far more pressing question. "Was it *you* who killed Amy? And Tina?"

Mark was still smiling, his teeth stained crimson. "Oh, yes. I killed them. And that punk who was harassing you in town. And I just got done killing Russ, too."

Helen's heart sank. For just a moment, she had hoped that Mark wasn't really the psychopath who had been terrorising the town. But now he was admitting it, and he was telling her that he'd killed Russ, too. She didn't understand why he would do such a thing. "Why would you want to kill people? It doesn't make any sense."

"Maybe I'm just psychotic. Maybe I enjoy hurting people. Maybe I've seen one too many video nasties. Maybe I thought it might be fun to make a video nasty of my own." He laughed once again, coughing up more blood.

He didn't have long left to live.

This was insane. Was Mark saying he'd been influenced by horror films? Was he saying they'd driven him insane? That just wasn't possible, was it? "But you weren't going to kill me?"

Mark shook his head. "No. Not yet, anyway. It's not your time to die just yet."

"What do you mean?"

"You still need to die."

"But you can't kill me now, can you?" said Helen, a sudden coldness filling her. She realised that she had been feeling almost sympathetic towards Mark. But he was a murderer. He'd tried to kill *her*. He didn't deserve any sympathy. "*I* killed *you*. It's over."

Mark was laughing once again then. So much blood. "This isn't over. Far from it. He's still coming. They're already here."

"Who's coming? Who's already here?"

"Them."

"Who's *them*?"

"They won't stop until the fires of hell consume the earth. That is all we desire."

Helen could feel herself growing more frantic. She'd had enough of all this nonsense. "What the fuck are you talking about?" she said. "Who is *them*?"

"You can't stop this. Your time will come." Mark gasped, his final breath escaping his lungs.

"Mark?" Helen shook him by the shoulder, not expecting any kind of reaction. "Mark? Mark?"

"Hey!" called a voice from somewhere up the street. "What the hell's goin' on out here?"

"Call the police!" shouted Helen, not bothering to look at whoever it was she was talking to. "And… and… and an ambulance!"

"Is he dead? Did you kill him?"

"Just *fucking* call them! Now!"

The voice said nothing more. Helen sat there in the street, sobbing, as blood pooled around Mark's corpse, and soaked into the torn knees of her jeans.

--- --- --- --- --- --- --- --- --- --- --- ---

People watch these movies purely for entertainment. There's nothing sinister about them. If you were to tell me that somebody went schizo and butchered a bunch of people, and *that they were fans of violent slasher movies, then I'd tell you that those two things are purely coincidental. These films aren't evil. The people who make them aren't evil. Of course, there is evil in this world, and it's right that we should want to eradicate it. But to suggest that* Cannibal Ferox *or* Mardi Gras Massacre *is to blame is nothing short of preposterous. Evil people do evil things; it's as simple as that.*

David Copley, entertainment journalist
and writer for 'Video News Weekly'

Chapter Nine:

Terror

Wendy picked Helen up from the police station just after nine that evening. When she had answered the telephone to a man informing her that he was with the police, she had immediately assumed that he was about to tell her that Helen was dead. Her heart had frozen and shattered into a million icy shards before he'd even said the words. When he had told her that, in actual fact, Helen was okay, she had almost collapsed, the relief overwhelming her motor functions. But she had steadied herself on the hallway wall and had listened as the officer – he had introduced himself as DCI Hanbury – gave her a shortened version of the story that Helen had told them. They had taken her statement, she hadn't done anything wrong, she'd killed the boy in self-defence, now she was free to go home.

The moment Wendy had seen Helen emerge into the reception of the police station, she had run to her, her arms wide, and wrapped her in the warmest hug she could muster. Helen broke down then, floods of tears bursting from her like a broken water main. "I thought he was going to kill me, mom!" she said, her sobs muddying the words to the point that they were almost unintelligible. But that didn't matter to Wendy; she just wanted to protect her daughter as best she could. "I thought I was going to die!"

"Shhhh…" said Wendy, stroking Helen's hair. "It's okay. I've got you. Nothing's going to hurt you now."

Wendy didn't like the thought, but there was no avoiding the fact that Helen was now just like her; she was a survivor. Like her, she had been forced to kill the maniac who was trying to kill her. Wendy never said it aloud, but she knew the trauma of those events, despite their having occurred so long ago now, had really fucked her up. She could only hope that this wouldn't have the same effect on Helen.

They drove home in silence. Helen didn't want to talk, not yet. Wendy understood. She'd felt the same on that night when she had killed George Milton. After that, the whole thing just played over and over in her head. For a long time she considered if there was anything she could've done differently, to prevent what had happened from happening. There wasn't, of course; how was she to have known that a psychopath had escaped from the local asylum?

But Helen would be thinking the same thing now. In her case, she had known the killer. Perhaps there *was* something she could've done. Perhaps there was some way she *could've* known what that boy was capable of. Wendy would never say this to her, of course, and if Helen ever brought it up herself, then Wendy would simply tell her that, no – there was absolutely no way she could've known.

Back at home, Wendy had made Helen a cup of tea and they had finally talked about what had happened.

Helen had apologised for the things she'd said before she'd left the house. She didn't want to fight with Wendy anymore. That suited Wendy just fine. Helen had explained how she'd intended to head home, but that she saw somebody following her. As is so happened, that somebody was one of her friends – a boy named Mark. It was he who had killed Amy and that other girl. He'd killed that boy last night, and they'd since found another body. Anyway, he chased Helen down an alley. They'd fought and she'd managed to escape. But he chased her again, and they fought some more. She managed to get a hold of his knife and had stabbed him twice, both times in the chest. He'd bled to death almost instantly. No surprise; Helen had managed to slice open his left ventricle.

As horrific as it was, Wendy was glad Helen had killed him. She was glad that Helen had fought back, and that she hadn't just rolled over and taken the cards she was being dealt. She was strong. She was brave. Wendy was so proud of her.

Helen had gone to bed soon after. When Wendy had gone to check on her, she'd been fast asleep, no doubt exhausted.

Good. She needed the rest.

The following morning, Helen awoke slightly later than usual. When she came downstairs, dressed in the oversized *Culture Club* t-shirt she always wore to bed, Wendy was in the kitchen, making herself toast. "Good morning, sweetheart," she said, offering Helen a warm smile. "Do you want something to eat?"

"Erm… Yeah, actually," said Helen. "I'm starving. I feel like I haven't eaten in months."

"You want some toast?"

"Yes please."

"Coming right up."

Helen sat at the breakfast table. Wendy grilled two slices of bread, then slathered them both in butter. "How are you feeling this morning?" she asked, as she placed the plate before Helen.

"Good, I think," said Helen, nodding her head. "I'm okay now."

Wendy shook her head. "I'm not so sure," she said, looking over her daughter, noting her pale complexion and the dark circles under her eyes. "You might be in shock."

Helen smiled. "I'm fine, mom. Honestly. I'm okay."

Wendy looked into Helen's eyes, trying to read her mind, trying to understand just how she really felt. There was a knock at the door then, breaking her concentration. She left Helen at the table, snacking on her toast, while she went to answer the door.

When she opened the door, she found Helen's friends Anna and Lorraine there. "Hi," said Lorraine, offering a sympathetic smile. "Is Helen home?"

Wendy sighed. She didn't think Helen was in the right state of mind to be seeing her friends right now. This boy she'd killed – who'd tried to kill *her* – he was supposed to be her friend, too. And if there was any doubt that Helen should've known that this boy was psychotic, then perhaps her other friends should've known too. "I'm sorry, girls," Wendy said, offering her own smile in return. "I'm not sure it's a good idea for you to see Helen today. She's been through a lot."

"No, Mom," said Helen, from partway along the hall. Wendy hadn't heard her leave the kitchen. "It's okay. I want to see them." She reached past Wendy and pulled the door open. "Come on in."

"Are you sure, Helen? You think this is a good idea?"

"Yes, Mom. I'm sure."

"Are you coming to college today?" Anna asked.

Helen nodded. "Yeah. I just need to get changed."

"Yeah," laughed Lorraine. "I don't think the school is too keen on *Boy George*."

"You're really going to college today?" Wendy interjected, hoping to convey that she didn't think it was wise. She knew everybody would be talking about Helen. There'd be so many questions. It might drag up painful memories.

"Yeah," said Helen, smiling, almost looking normal. "Honestly, Mom, I'm fine. I just want things to get back to normal as soon as possible."

"But…"

"And you don't have to worry. I'm safe now. Nobody is going to try and hurt me anymore."

"That's right," agreed Lorraine. "This one's a tough cookie. And besides, we've got her back!"

Helen laughed. It was almost as if nothing had even happened, as if there wasn't even a trace of trauma within her. "Okay," said Wendy, reluctantly. "But if you have any problems, I want you to come straight home, okay? I've got a shift at work today, but if you need me, just call."

"You got it," said Helen. She, Lorraine and Anna then headed up the stairs and into Helen's room.

Wendy returned to the kitchen. She couldn't help but think back to when she was a girl. The day after the massacre, she hadn't wanted to leave the house. She hadn't wanted to leave her bed. She was terrified that somebody might be out there, waiting to kill her. She was *still* terrified. But that didn't mean Helen had to feel the same. Perhaps it was good that she didn't, and that she could just pretend like nothing had even happened. Perhaps she was strong.

Perhaps she was stronger than Wendy ever was.

—

"So," said Lorraine, slumping back on Helen's bed, making herself comfortable. "What *really* happened?"

"What do you mean?" said Helen, pulling the t-shirt off over her head and tossing it beside the bed. She, Lorraine and Anna had seen each other naked a million times before, she wasn't going to start worrying about it now.

"Was it really Mark?"

Helen nodded her head. "Yes. It was."

"And he tried to kill you?"

Helen nodded again.

Anna puffed out her cheeks and shook her head. "That's fucked up. And it was him that killed Tina? And Amy?"

Once again, Helen nodded. "And that other kid." She thought for a moment, wondering if they'd heard about what happened to Russ. "And Russ, too," she said.

"I know! We saw Ryan just before we came here. He's devastated."

"So, were you *with* Mark last night?" asked Lorraine.

"Was I *with* him?" said Helen, seeking clarification.

"Yeah. You know. Like, were you and him… you know…"

Helen frowned as if the idea was disgusting to her. But the truth was, she'd considered it a lot last night. She had liked Mark. He'd been kind to her. He was always friendly. He was funny and charming. Yes – she had imagined them dating at some point in the not-too-distant future…

Shit.

How fucked up did that make her, wanting to date a serial killer?

Of course, had she known he was psychotic, then she almost certainly *wouldn't* have wanted to date him.

"No," Helen confirmed. "I wasn't *with* him. He followed me. He attacked me. He tried to kill me. So, I fought him, I got his knife, and I killed him first."

Lorraine scoffed, disgusted. "And he didn't tell you why?"

Helen shook her head. "No, he didn't."

She hadn't told anybody what Mark had said in his dying breaths, not even the police. It was insane. Most of what he'd said didn't even make any sense. And more to the point, Helen didn't even want to think about it herself.

Dressed now, Helen, Anna and Lorraine made their way back down the stairs. Helen's mother was waiting for her there. "Are sure you're going to be okay?" she asked, reaching out and gently stroking Helen's face.

"Yes, Mom," Helen insisted, "I'll be fine."

"I still worry about you, you know."

"There's nothing for you to worry about. The killer is dead. We're safe now."

Helen's mother smiled. She nodded her head, as tears seemed to fill her eyes. "I know you are. Okay. Have a good day then. And remember, if you need me, just call."

"Okay. Will do." Helen kissed her mother on the cheek before ushering Lorraine and Anna out of the house, and closing the door behind her.

As they walked along the street, Anna and Lorraine chatted nonchalantly between themselves. Helen remained silent, lost in her thoughts. In the daylight now, the streets looked pleasant. Although it was still cool out, the sun was shining, giving everything an almost gratifying aura. She dared not think about the pool of blood that no doubt stained the tarmac just a few streets away from where they now walked. But she thought about Mark, and the things he'd done, the things he'd said. Why had he tried to kill her? And how had she not seen it coming. Surely it should be quite easy to spot a psychopath. How was Mark able to hide it so well, to trick her into thinking that he cared about her?

"Helloooo?" said Anna. "Earth to Helen? You in there?"

Suddenly, Helen understood that Anna had been speaking to her, and that she'd been so far zoned out that she hadn't even noticed. "I'm sorry," she said, "what did you say?"

"I said – I hope we're still on for the party."

"The party?" Helen said, somewhat confused.

"Yeah. The Halloween party. It's on Friday, remember?"

Helen *hadn't* remembered. It had entirely slipped her mind. It was the last thing she really wanted to be thinking about right now. "Oh," she said, the memory finally coming back to her. "Right. Yeah."

"Hold up," said Lorraine, her hand pressed against Helen's tummy, stopping her in her tracks. "You don't sound too sure. Please tell me you're still coming."

Helen sighed and shook her head. "I don't know," she said, her eyes fixed on the ground at her feet. "I did nearly die last night, remember? I'm tired. I just don't really feel in the mood."

"No, no, no. You *have* to come. You *need* to come. It'll be good for you. It'll take your mind off everything."

"Lorraine's right!" said Anna, nodding her head like an over-enthusiastic puppy. "You've gotta get out of that house! You know we'll look after you, right? And, well, Mark's dead. The killer is no longer with us."

"Yeah, I know," said Helen, looking up now, and into the eyes of her two best friends. "I just… I'm not sure I can cope with all the eyes on me. I don't like being the centre of attention. Maybe my mom was right. Maybe I should stay at home."

Lorraine shook her head. "Listen," she said, taking Helen's hands in her own. "You should do whatever feels right to you. But this party – it won't be the same if you're not there. We both *really* want you to come."

"Yeah," agreed Anna. "She's right, you know?"

Helen smiled, the kindness of her friends actually touching her. "Alright. Fine. I'll come."

"Yay!" cheered Lorraine, almost sarcastically. "I knew you'd change your mind. You can't resist a good party. You're a party animal!"

Helen laughed, rolling her eyes at the irony, being that she wasn't really a fan of parties at all. "Oh, yeah," she said, the sarcasm practically dripping from the tip of her tongue. "A party animal. That's me alright."

A little closer to the college, and the three girls eventually met up with Chris and Ryan. They were sharing a joint, a thick white blanket of smoke almost obscuring them from view. As they approached, Chris looped his arms around Lorraine's neck and pulled her in close, kissing her deep.

"Hey, Helen," Ryan said, offering the warmest smile he could seemingly manage. "How's it going after last night?"

"I'm okay," said Helen. "I've been better, I guess."

"Yeah, I'm sure you have. Listen – I just wanted to tell you how sorry I am. How sorry *we all* are. Mark was our friend. We should've known that he was a lunatic."

"I was his friend too. I didn't see it. You weren't to know."

Ryan nodded his head, seemingly satisfied by her response. He sucked in a long draw of his spliff. Despite his sometimes heartless nature, right now Ryan seemed to be devastated.

"How are *you* doing?" said Helen, repeating Ryan's earlier question, but directing it back to him. "You heard about Russ, right? I know he was your friend."

Ryan nodded. “I can’t believe he’s dead. It’s fucking bullshit. I don’t get why Mark would’ve done this. He must’ve been really fucked in the head.”

“I think he was,” said Helen, sympathetically.

“Well, anyway,” said Ryan, dropping the last of the joint and extinguishing it underfoot. “I never did return this tape.” He pulled the copy of *Driller Killer* that he’d borrowed the other day out of his bag. “I thought I might go and drop it off at the shop. I know that’d make Russ happy. Plus, leaving a video nasty on his doorstep might seem like a big ‘fuck you’ to the world. I know he’d find that funny.”

Helen smiled. Ryan wasn’t normally so sentimental. “That’s a good idea. Come on – we’ll all go.”

They made their way through to the shopping centre, only to find that a small crowd had once again formed outside the video shop. It wasn’t as big as the crowd had been when they had originally arrested Russ, but there were a handful of people congregating around the area. To some extent, this disgusted Helen; more people had been there, ready to watch Russ burn, than were there now to offer their sympathies. The same journalist and cameraman were there once again, as was the politician – Gary Smart. With him now was a woman that, as she had done with Gary, Helen recognised from the TV. She was old and frail looking, with curly white hair, and plastic framed spectacles.

This lady was Margaret Whitehead – the spokeswoman for the group who were campaigning for tighter censorship laws, and the permanent banning of the video nasties. It seemed as if she was on the news every other day, giving lectures in morality, and pretty much telling people that they were going to hell.

“With me now is Margaret Whitehead,” said the journalist, introducing the elderly lady standing before him. “The author of ‘Violence On Video: The End Of Morality?’, and a leading campaigner in the effort to have the video nasties banned. Mrs. Whitehead, thank you for joining us.”

“It’s my pleasure,” the old lady smiled, showing off her perfectly white teeth, in what must’ve been a fairly new set of dentures.

"Please," the journalist continued, "give us your thoughts on what has transpired here in the last twenty-four hours."

"Well, I think it's quite clear what has transpired here, these grotesque 'video nasties' have caused the deaths of what I understand to be five people now, including the murderer himself."

"So, you put that down solely to the video nasties?"

"Oh, I'm sure there were lots of factors that played into what happened here. But, as you can see right now, the reason we are outside this video rental shop is because the proprietor — who is now dead — had continued to distribute these movies, despite their prohibition. As I understand it, one of his customers was the killer."

The journalist turned to Gary Smart. "You were here yesterday," he said. "You seemed to believe that, based on his access to video nasties, the proprietor of this store was actually the killer. He, of course, has now become a victim. Is it possible that this idea — that horror movies can cause people to become deranged psychopaths — is actually false?"

"No, I don't think that is the case. Of course, mistakes were made here, but the fact remains that the perpetrator of these heinous crimes was a fan of video nasties, and the proprietor of this shop was the one who facilitated his viewing of them. If anything, he is just as much to blame for this horrifying string of murders as the murderer is himself."

This angered Helen. Mark didn't kill Amy and Tina because he'd been watching video nasties. He did it because he was mentally ill. He was a psychopath; it was as simple as that.

Ryan wasn't happy about this either. Helen could tell by the reddening of his cheeks that he didn't like them speaking ill of Russ, when the truth was that he'd done nothing wrong. He turned and walked away, muttering about how everything was fucked, and how all of this was bullshit. The others followed.

But Helen remained for a few moments more, listening as the journalist finished up his report.

"Do you think this validates your claims?" the journalist asked Margaret. "Do you think this will provide another step towards getting these movies banned?"

"I think it *has* to," Margaret confirmed. "This is exactly what we *knew* would happen. We've tried to warn people. These movies can make people sick. They can cause the horrific scenes we have watched playout here. We must put a stop to this reign of terror."

--- --- --- --- --- --- --- --- --- --- --- ---

Mark my words – the day will come when these movies have such a profoundly negative effect on somebody, that they will drive them to kill. There's nothing we can do to stop this. We must get these vile videos off the shelves, and out of the hands of our children. Tell me – what do we get from these films? Films such as The Hills Have Eyes *and* I Spit On Your Grave *all glorify rape and torture and violent murder. What good can come from movies such as these? If it were up to me, I'd be trying to prevent these movies from being made in the first place.*

Margret Whitehead, conservative activist and author of

'Violence On Video: The End Of Morality?'

CHAPTER TEN:

MADHOUSE

Not much happened over the course of the next two days. Helen did her best to forget about the horrors that had afflicted her. By the time Friday rolled around, she had practically forgotten what day it was, the past forty-eight hours being little more than a blur. She'd forgotten that the party was that night.

She'd also forgotten that it was Halloween.

But Lorraine soon reminded her. "So," she said as she, Anna and Helen walked towards the college, their arms linked, "what are you wearing tonight?"

"Tonight?" said Helen, somewhat confused.

"Yeah. Tonight. The party."

"Oh, shit," Helen said, once again feeling as though she wasn't in the mood for a party. Far from it, in all honesty. "I forgot."

"Well, I don't care. You said you were coming. You can't back out now."

"Honestly, I don't feel like it. I'm tired. I need to get some sleep."

"Tough shit. You can sleep when you're dead."

Helen frowned at Lorraine, hoping to convey the sentiment that such a statement wasn't entirely appropriate just yet – it was still too soon.

"Sorry," said Lorraine, realising her mistake. "But… Whatever… You're coming."

"Yeah," said Anna. "You *have* to come. I don't want to be stuck as a third wheel to Lorraine and Chris."

"I'm sure Ryan would look after you," chuckled Helen.

"Oh, great. Stuck with that stoner. That's just what I need."

Helen shook her head. "I don't have a costume anyway."

"That's okay," said Lorraine. "I'm going as a zombie bride. We can make you into my bridesmaid. I've got a dress you can wear. We'll just sew some patches onto it, and – voila!"

Helen couldn't help but be amused by Lorraine's enthusiasm. "Ugghh… Okay! I'll come!"

"Fabulous!" laughed Lorraine. "It's gonna be great!"

"I don't think I'm going to tell my mom, though. I think she'd still freak out."

"What?" said Anna. "Even though Mark's dead? She wouldn't be thinking that somebody else might be out there waiting to kill you, would she?"

"I wouldn't put anything past her, to be honest. She *is* crazy, remember?"

The three girls were laughing then, as they made their way into college. The news vans were still loitering outside the campus. Over the past few days, Margaret Whitehead had visited numerous places in town, followed by an entourage of journalists, all enraptured by her thoughts on the video nasties and the violence they'd caused to unfold in this town.

Helen had done her best to ignore it.

As promised, Helen didn't tell her mother where she was going that evening. She hadn't remembered, but her mother was off to her book club that evening – just as she did every Friday. By around six p.m., she was packing her bag and collecting up whatever paperback she'd been reading over the course of the last fortnight. She pulled on her coat, and approached Helen who was now sitting on the sofa in the living room, reading a book of her own. "You should come to book club with me one day," Helen's mother said, smiling enthusiastically. "I think you'd enjoy it."

Helen smiled in return. "I don't think you guys read the same sorts of books as me." Helen turned her book over to display the cover of the book she was reading – Stephen King's *The Shining*. Although she didn't really like horror films, horror literature was a different thing entirely.

"Well," her mother said, "you could always try reading something different."

"Yeah. Maybe I will someday."

"Anyway… what are you up to this evening?"

"Oh, nothing. Just gonna read a few more chapters, then probably watch some TV." Helen neglected to mention the fact that she was actually off out to the forbidden Halloween party. Her mother would not have been happy if she knew.

"Why don't you come with me tonight?" Helen's mother said, a pleasant grin on her face. It was nice to see her happy for a change. Book club was one of the few times she ever left the house, and it was one of the only things that she truly enjoyed. But sitting around talking about literature wasn't exactly Helen's idea of a good time.

"No thanks," chuckled Helen. "I think I'll pass."

"All right, then. Well, I'm off now, so I'll see you later. I should be back by ten."

"Okay," said Helen. "Have fun."

And with that, her mother left the house, locking the door behind her.

As soon as she was gone, Helen stood from the sofa and hurried across to the living room window, just in time to see her mother backing the car out of the driveway, and disappearing along the street. She then slipped on her pumps and pulled on her jacket. She used her own key to unlock the door from the inside, then stepped out into the cool autumn air, pausing momentarily to consider the fact that she was indeed safe, and that the killer who had once posed a threat was no more. It still hurt to think that Mark might've wanted her dead, but she had so far managed to bury that feeling deep in the pit of her stomach.

She closed the door and locked it once again, then set off for Lorraine's house.

Ten minutes later, and she had arrived. Anna was already there. The two of them had already started drinking, Anna having stolen a bottle of vodka from her mother's drinks cabinet. They'd mixed the vile alcohol with Diet Coke, just to make it taste a little more pleasant. The moment that Helen was inside, Lorraine was thrusting a glass of the same noxious beverage into her hand. "Drink up," said Lorraine. "We're already running late."

Helen looked both Lorraine and Anna over. They were already dressed in their costumes. Lorraine wore a white dress, torn ragged, the front ripped open then crudely stitched back together, so as to reveal a healthy dose of cleavage. Anna wore a green dress with green elasticated wings.

"Okay, okay," said Helen, sipping at her drink, almost wincing as the sour taste hit her tastebuds. "Did you sort out a dress for me?"

"Yep," said Lorraine, kneeling onto the sofa and reaching behind it. When she returned, she brought with her another white dress, to which she had crudely sewn strips of torn, brown material. She held it up before herself. "Perfect," she said. "You'll make a beautiful bridesmaid."

"Thanks," said Helen taking the dress from her.

"Go get changed then," said Anna, bouncing excitedly on the spot. "We need to get going."

Helen rolled her eyes. She didn't see what the rush was. Still, she tipped her head back and swallowed the last of her drink in one gulp. She then made her way to Lorraine's downstairs bathroom and changed into her dress. Then, back in the lounge, Anna applied make up to her face; black smudges beneath her eyes, making her an almost mirror image of Lorraine.

Another drink, and the three girls were ready to go. The honk of a car horn from outside informed Lorraine that their lift had arrived.

“Who’s that?” asked Helen, peering out of the front window at the battered old Ford that now sat at the end of the driveway.

“That’s Pete,” Lorraine confirmed, “Chris’ brother. He’s giving us a lift.”

“So, where’s Chris?” Helen was confused as to why he wouldn’t have been there.

“He and Ryan went early.”

“So they’ll be hammered by the time we get there!” Anna laughed hysterically.

Helen rolled her eyes. “Looks like they won’t be the only ones…” she said, her accusatory tone aimed in Anna’s direction.

“Oh, fuck you! Just ‘cause I’m ready to party!”

Laughing, the girls left the house and climbed into Pete’s car. “Thanks for the ride,” Lorraine said, settling herself back into the passenger seat.

“No problem,” said Pete. Helen couldn’t remember ever having seen him before. Come to think of it, she hadn’t actually known that Chris *had* a brother. He was quite a handsome guy, with thick stubble and wavy blonde hair. “You’ll have to find your own way home though; I’ve got a date tonight.”

“Oooh,” laughed Lorraine, “who’s the lucky lady?”

“Nobody you know,” said Pete, pulling his car away from the curb.

Just on the outskirts of town, the concrete and pavement of the buildings and roads quickly dissolved into the soft greens and browns of the countryside. The road on which the car was driving was lined on both sides by tall rows of corn, the tarmac having carved a snaking path through the yellow vegetation. The moon above was full, a harsh white sheen bathing the earth. But the path ahead was nothing but black, the headlights slicing through the darkness, Pete driving much quicker than he really ought to be, taking each corner much sharper than Helen really deemed to be safe.

But then they were there; an opening in the corn led through a gate, and onto a dirt road, the mud churned up by the tyres of the industrial machinery that had driven there previously.

Pete didn't drive down this path, however. Instead, he parked up at the side of the road, and ushered the girls out.

"Can't you drop us off at the actual place?" Lorraine complained.

"No," said Pete, bluntly. "I just got my car cleaned. And besides, you should be grateful I even brought you out here at all."

"Yeah. Whatever. Okay. Thanks." Lorraine climbed out of the car.

Helen followed. Once she was out, and having helped the already heavily intoxicated Anna out too, she leant back into the car. "Thank you," she said, offering Pete a kind smile.

"Sure. No problem." Pete nodded his head. Helen closed the car door, then Pete was gone.

A number of people, all dressed in Halloween costumes of some description, were already heading along the dirt path. Helen urged the other two girls to follow them. Following the lead of somebody dressed as a ghost – Helen had no idea who this was, what with the white sheet draped over their head, dragging on the floor all the way past their feet – they finally arrived at the slaughterhouse.

Loud music played from inside, flashing lights, a myriad of colours, blinking on and off in the various windows, and the doors sitting slightly ajar. From the outside, the building looked like any other industrial agricultural building. But when Helen entered the building, she was taken aback by the effort that had been put into this year's decorations.

Nobody knew who did it. There were rumours that the party had actually been organised – and *paid* for – each year by some of the town's adults, those who never really wanted the annual party to have been cancelled ever since the massacre. But the truth was, it was most likely the older kids who did it. Like Helen and her friends, they too had probably been kept in the dark about who *actually* organised the party, until they themselves had become the ones who needed to organise it (the previous organisers likely having aged-out, having moved out of town, or gotten married and had kids).

Blankets of faux cobwebs adorned the walls and hung from the ceilings, plastic spiders interweaved with the stretched wool. Plastic skeletons hung from the ceiling, ropes tied into nooses and hung around their necks. Rubber bats bounced on elastic strings. Numerous pumpkins had been carved into jack-o'-lanterns, candles flickering at the backs of their throats, each with some variation on the typical 'scary' face; crooked eyes and pointed teeth.

The main area where the party took place was the same hall in which the hundreds of animals who had been slaughtered here would've once been held. A foul smell still hung in the air, despite the building not having housed any livestock for more than a decade. Helen imagined the stench might've been a lot worse back in those days. At the back of this hall, a stage had been erected, and on this stage, the DJ had set up his decks.

At the front of the stage, two television sets had been placed, one at each corner. The one to Helen's left was playing the movie *Driller Killer* – a man with long, unkempt hair bathed in a shower of blood, the screen filled with red. The TV to the right played the movie *I Spit On Your Grave* – a man and a woman shared a bathtub, before the woman promptly sliced off the man's penis, the ensuing spray of blood coating the walls in crimson.

"Hey sexy ladies!" slurred Chris, as he wrapped his arms around Lorraine's waist and pulled her in tight, kissing her long and deep, practically dry humping her. When he finally removed his tongue from her throat, he turned to Helen and Anna. "Who wants a drink?"

"I thought you'd never ask!" giggled Anna.

"It's like a madhouse in here," Helen remarked.

"I know!" said Chris, enthusiastically. "Cool, right?"

Helen rolled her eyes. "Yeah. Real cool."

Chris led them to the back of the hall, where numerous bottles of spirits and mixers had been stacked onto a picnic table.

Lorraine poured their drinks – too much vodka, not enough cola – and then they made their way to the dancefloor.

—

Gary had never seen anything like it. He almost couldn't believe his eyes.

Actually, he could. These kids were Goddamned degenerates. The nerve of them. After everything that had gone on this past week, somehow they still thought *this* was appropriate. Looking at these kids – it was difficult to get a fix on their age, what with them all being dressed up in Halloween costumes, but they all appeared to be teenagers – it stood every possibility that it was *their* friends who had been murdered. Even if they weren't friends, they were probably acquaintances – a friend of a friend, that kind of thing.

Either way, this was certainly in bad taste. Many of them were stumbling around, completely drunk. And some of the girls were barely wearing any clothing, their legs and their breasts on show! It was no wonder this country was going down the shitter.

And what even was this place? A farm, perhaps? It was a large agricultural building of some kind. Gary wasn't really familiar with this sort of thing, what with his being born and raised in the city. It looked like a large barn, all wood and rusted iron. Whatever it was, it looked as if it had been abandoned for some time. Perhaps it was a slaughterhouse. How inappropriate would that be? These kids were sick in the head.

From his position, hidden in the darkness of the adjoining field, Gary watched as dozens of partygoers flooded into the building. Loud music emanated from inside, disco lights flashing through the windows, red and green and yellow. He'd spotted a group of the teenagers out on the main road, as he'd been driving past. Their costumes had made them stand out like a sore thumb – one was dressed as Count Dracula; another was wrapped in bandages like a mummy; one of the girls was dressed as a cheerleader, although her outfit was splattered with fake blood. In his short time in this town, he'd learned all about the massacre that had taken place here two decades ago. It was actually Margaret Whitehead – what an incredible woman *she* was! – who had provided all the details. She'd told him that, ever since the massacre, the town's annual Halloween party had been prohibited. That was how Gary had been sure that these kids were up to no good.

As such, he'd followed them. He parked his car into a lay-by, then cut through the fields of corn, following the raucous sound of the intoxicated youths.

There must've been at least two hundred of them in there. Gary wasn't sure they were doing anything illegal – the prohibition of the party was surely something that couldn't be upheld by law. But if they were trespassing on this property, then the least the police could do would be to break up this little shindig, and send these little bastards home. Maybe they might arrest whoever had organised this party, and string them up as a deterrent. Even if no laws *had* been broken, this was still entirely immoral.

Yes, he'd drive to the nearest police station and tell them what was going on. And then, he'd be sure to inform Margret of what he'd found, and what he'd done to fix the problem. That was sure to earn him some decent brownie points. If he could garner support from her – as he already supported her in everything that she was fighting for – then that would almost certainly lead to his appointment to a higher position in the prime minister's cabinet. Who knows; maybe he might even be able to look to become PM himself.

An excitement itched in Gary's stomach. He couldn't wait to speak to Margaret, to accept the praise she was sure to heap upon him. He turned, and…

There was a man behind him.

Gary didn't get a chance to look at him too closely. Not that there was much to see; the man was dressed all in black, and he wore a black balaclava over his face.

Gary's heart leapt into his throat. He was about to say something when he noticed the hammer that the man was holding. He was about to scream then, but the man cut the sound short with a swift blow to the side of Gary's head.

Gary felt his skull crack. He *heard* the bone splintering, directly in his ear. A warm numbness emanated from the point of impact. He raised his hand to the side of his head and felt where the blow had landed. The side of his head almost felt as if it were now concave, and where his fingertips ran through his hair, they came away warm and sticky. He looked at his fingers. They were coated in a layer of blood.

The man stood and watched as a peculiar weakness overcame Gary. His legs gave out from under him and he fell to the ground. His breathing was shallow, each breath accompanied by an odd snore, wet at the back of his throat, almost as if he were choking. The man dropped to his knees beside Gary, hammer raised overhead. He then brought the hammer down, over and over, until the skin of Gary's forehead finally split open, skull splintered, brain leaking out through the newly opened orifice.

Gary's killer then stood, shaking the hammer downward, the sudden movement knocking loose the clump of bloody meat and hair that had adhered there. He stepped over the corpse, leaving it there in the corn field, hidden from sight.

--- --- --- --- --- --- --- --- --- --- --- ---

People may accuse us of being overprotective. But since when did that become a bad thing? Why take any risks? We know what the studies show – the results have not been good. Today's children are already subjected to far too much immorality – sex, alcohol, drugs, pornography. We do not need to exasperate the dire situation with which we are faced, by adding these grotesque exploitation movies into the mix. We're just adding fuel to the fire. I want to protect our children. For their safety as much as our own, we need to put a stop to this. I, for one, do not want to become a victim.

Gary Smart, conservative MP and

campaigner against social liberalism

CHAPTER ELEVEN:

DEMENTED

The abattoir's holding pen – the wide area just before the stage, still surrounded by iron gates, the protective layer of paint now peeling away from the metallic substrate – had been repurposed into a makeshift dance floor, just as it had every year. It was here that the majority of the partygoers were congregated, all squashed in together, a writhing mass of humanity, bouncing up and down, shoulder to shoulder. Helen was amongst them. She and Anna were dancing together, while Lorraine and Chris were dancing beside them, wrapped up in each other's arms.

"Where's Ryan?" asked Helen, nodding towards Chris, hoping to let him know that this question was directed towards him. Her voice was raised, so as to be heard over the deafening sound of Pete Burns blasting through the lyrics of *You Spin Me Round.*

"No idea," said Chris, shrugging his shoulders. "He said he was going to go smoke a joint, and I haven't seen him since."

"When was that?" Helen shook her head, her vocal cords straining.

"I don't know. Half an hour ago, maybe."

"Why are you so worried about Ryan anyway?" chuckled Anna. "You wanna fuck him?"

Helen could feel herself frowning. She knew Anna was drunk, but even so, it wasn't like her to be so crude. And besides, the answer to her question was no – definitely not. But still, there was an uncomfortable feeling in her gut, telling her that it wasn't wise for them to be going their separate ways. It was a stupid feeling, she knew that. Mark was dead; he posed no further threat to anybody. But still, she couldn't shake the feeling that something wasn't right. "No," she said. "I was just curious, is all. It's not like him to miss a party."

"Well, I'm sure he's fine. And anyway, looks like you've already got an admirer here."

Puzzled, Helen followed Anna's gaze to the other side of the hall. There, Kevin – the infamous ex-boyfriend – was watching her, swigging from a bottle of beer.

"Oh, great," sighed Helen. "That's all I need."

Anna laughed. "Well, at least you've got a couple of options for who gets to take you home tonight: Kevin or Ryan?"

"Trust me, I won't be leaving with either of them."

"You should make them fight for your affections! The winner gets to take you home!"

Helen laughed, as Anna clapped her hands together excitedly. For a moment, she wasn't sure if Anna was serious or not. Not that it mattered either way. "I'm telling you now – *neither* of them gets to take me home tonight. If I try to leave with either of them, do me a favour and shoot me, okay? And besides, we can't very well get Ryan to fight if we don't know where he is, can we?"

—

Ryan rolled the flint of his lighter over with his thumb, sparking the flame to life. He held it up to the joint he held between his lips and inhaled deeply, filling his lungs with that sweet marijuana smoke. He held it in, then exhaled, the ensuing cloud dancing its way up towards the cloudless sky, momentarily obscuring the stars above.

He had found himself a spot out the back of the slaughterhouse, out of the way of prying eyes. Not that he really cared if people saw him; everybody knew he was a stoner already. Nobody was likely to tell him that he shouldn't be doing this. No – of more concern to him was the fact that, should anybody see him, they were likely to ask if they might join him. And it wasn't like they'd have their own weed to smoke; they'd expect him to share. And again, it wasn't as if Ryan would normally mind sharing, but his supply was running low. Since Russ had been killed, he hadn't yet had chance to find a different supplier to buy from.

That was a pretty callous way of thinking about it. Russ wasn't just his drug dealer; he was a friend. It had broken his heart when he found out that Russ had died. He managed to hide his emotions well, but the truth was, once he'd gotten home from college that day, he'd broken down in tears. Russ was a good guy. He hadn't deserved to die. Ryan would certainly miss him.

But the fact remained that Ryan currently had nobody else from whom to buy his weed, and what remained of the last half-ounce he'd bought might only suffice for the next few days.

Fuck it. There must've been loads of people he could buy from. He'd ask around at college next week.

Ryan took another deep draw on his spliff, the warmth of the smoke as it filtered down his trachea comforting him. He was already somewhat drunk, having gotten through at least eight bottles of beer already. The fuzzy feeling the weed gave him only served to intensify the feeling of intoxication. It was a feeling that, at that precise moment, he was thoroughly enjoying.

At least, that *was* the case before the man had appeared behind him, striding across the yard towards him, axe in hand. The sight of this man – dressed all in black, his face obscured by some kind of mask – was enough to quickly sober Ryan up.

"What the fuck is this?" he muttered, as the man neared him.

Despite his seemingly instant sobriety, the cloudy state of his brain still wasn't allowing him to think properly. His initial thought had been that this was just another partygoer, the mask just a part of his costume. The axe was most likely made of rubber, right?

Wrong.

Only as the man raised the axe did the fear finally set in.

"No, no, no, no, no!" muttered Ryan, stumbling backwards, the joint tumbling from between his fingers. "Wait!"

But the man didn't wait. He swung the axe as if it were a baseball bat, and he was swinging for the fences. The blade of the axe chewed through Ryan's neck with ease, separating his vertebrae, sending his head tumbling to the ground, much like the smouldering spliff had just moments ago.

Ryan's body remained upright for just a few moments, blood squirting from his ruined arteries. But then it gave out, his legs collapsing out from under him, leaving his headless corpse no more than a crumpled heap in the dirt.

—

"Hey," said Kevin, as he approached Helen from behind.

His voice startled Helen. She hadn't expected him to be there, and Anna hadn't been around to provide any warning; she'd gone to get them all another drink. Of course, that must've been why Kevin had decided to take this opportunity to approach.

Helen turned and smiled. "Hey."

"How's it going?" Kevin asked awkwardly, not having much else to say, but clearly desperate to make some kind of conversation. "You enjoying the party?"

Helen shrugged her shoulders. "Yeah. It's okay, I guess. Same as every year, right?"

Kevin smiled. "I guess so."

Helen wasn't sure she wanted to be making conversation with him. He'd hurt her more than he'd ever truly know. But then again, what with everything that had occurred over the past week, she wasn't sure that holding grudges was the best thing to do.

"Listen," Kevin continued. "Do you think that maybe we could talk? Could we go somewhere a bit quieter?"

Before Helen could answer, Lorraine had pushed her way between her and Kevin. “Hey Kev,” she slurred. “I thought I told you to leave Helen alone.”

“Indeed, you did,” said Kevin, grinding his teeth, his disdain for Lorraine blatantly obvious. “I’m just trying to talk to her.”

“Well maybe she doesn’t want to talk to you!”

“It’s fine,” said Helen, hoping to diffuse the situation before it all kicked off. “Honestly. I don’t mind.”

“Can we go then?” asked Kevin.

Helen nodded. She looked back to Lorraine. “It’s okay. Honestly, I’m fine. We’re just going to go and talk. Okay?”

“Okay,” said Lorraine. “If that makes you happy. Just don’t fall for his apologies. Once a cheat, always a cheat.”

“Yeah. Okay. I got it.”

Lorraine scrunched up her face, almost as if she didn’t quite believe that she was allowing Helen to go anywhere with Kevin. Chris hooked his arm around her waist and pulled her aside. “Come on,” he said. “Let’s leave them to it.”

“Alright, fine,” said Lorraine, allowing Chris to drag her away. “Where’s Anna with my drink, anyway?”

Anna had gone to get the drinks. She’d be back momentarily; she just needed to use the bathroom first, her bladder feeling as if it were almost ready to explode.

Although the slaughterhouse had been disused for more than a decade, the plumbing still functioned as it had when the place had been operational. There was running water in the taps, and the toilets still flushed. The bathrooms were located at the end of a corridor, situated behind the staging area. The walls of this corridor were constructed from breeze blocks, making the area much colder than the rest of the building.

Anna stumbled her way down the hall, knowing that the very moment she got into the bathroom, she was likely to spew up her guts. She quickened her pace, not wanting to get caught short, and spray the walls with vomit. She pushed open the flimsy wooden door at the entrance to the bathroom, finding the room to be entirely empty. She made her way to the first cubical, pushed open the door, and dropped to her knees.

As predicted, she immediately puked.

She was too drunk. She ought to go home.

No. What she needed was another drink.

Even in her inebriated state, she knew that wasn't quite right. Those two things didn't quite align with one another. But what did she care? She'd come to the party to have a good time, and, up until this very moment, as her abdominal muscles constricted, wringing out the contents of her stomach like a saturated sponge, that was exactly what she had been doing. She'd no doubt regret drinking so much in the morning, but – fuck it – you only live once, right?

Sometimes, just *how long* you get to live is taken out of your hands.

As was the case for Anna herself.

She hadn't heard the bathroom door opening behind her. She hadn't noticed the man approaching her from behind, hadn't heard him over the sound of her vomit spattering the porcelain bowl of the toilet. She didn't even sense his presence as she sat upright, swiping her hair back over her head, wishing that she hadn't gotten so drunk, promising herself that she'd never drink again.

That was a promise she'd most certainly be keeping.

The man looped a length of chain around her neck and pulled it tight. He dragged Anna backwards, out of the cubicle. Her ankles rolled awkwardly under her own body weight, as her legs thrashed, trying to get some kind of purchase on the tiled floor. She clawed at the chain, but the man pulled harder, the steel links biting into her skin, crushing the cartilage of her trachea, rendering her ability to breathe all but null and void.

Anna wanted to scream. She couldn't. She couldn't even breath. She could feel her brain going numb, the oxygen in her blood depleting.

It took just a few more moments for her to lose consciousness.

Another moment, and she was dead.

—

"I really am sorry, you know?" said Kevin, as he and Helen walked the perimeter of the yard that fronted the slaughterhouse.

"Yeah," said Helen, putting up an invisible barrier. "You've already told me that."

"So then why won't you forgive me?"

Helen felt her eyebrows lower. "Seriously? You *cheated* on me. Why should I forgive you?"

"I know I did. But that wasn't meant to happen. It didn't mean anything. It just… sort of… happened."

"Yeah. I know. And because of that, I can't trust you anymore. And I can't be with somebody I don't trust."

"That sort of thing would never happen again. It was a stupid mistake."

"Yeah, one that cost us our relationship."

"But it doesn't have to be like this."

Helen scuffed her shoes through the dirt, leaving a trail behind herself. It was cold outside, but she'd drank enough alcohol that she barely noticed the gooseflesh rising on her arms. She was also drunk enough that she knew she might be about to forgive Kevin for what he'd done to her. She couldn't let that happen; she didn't want that, did she?

Kevin continued – "When I heard that you were attacked, and that you'd nearly died, I felt completely broken. I could never have forgiven myself for what I did, if I'd never gotten to apologise to you."

"Well," said Helen, hoping to sound dismissive. "Now you have, so you can rest easy."

"But that's not what I want."

Helen stopped. She turned to face Kevin, cutting him off. "So, what *do* you want?"

"I want us to be together again."

Helen almost wanted to laugh. She shook her head, denying the fact that, deep down, part of her wanted the same thing. But, no – she'd fight it. She wouldn't let that happen. She was better off alone. If she got back together with Kevin, he'd probably just cheat on her again. Her heart had already been broken enough. "That can't happen," she said.

"Why not?"

"Because I don't want it too. You really hurt me. I can't allow that to happen again."

Kevin stared at the ground, a sorrowful look on his face. Helen knew that he truly regretted what he'd done. And that was good; he deserved to feel that way. "So, where does that leave us?" Kevin asked, finally returning his gaze to Helen's eyes.

Helen sighed. "Look," she said. "I *can* forgive you… I *do* forgive you. But our relationship is over. I can't risk this happening again. I think I'm better off steering clear of boys altogether for a while."

Kevin offered a weak smile. Thankfully, he seemed to understand that there was nothing more he could say or do to rectify the situation. It was best just to let sleeping dogs lie. "So, can we still be friends?"

Helen offered a weak smile of her own. She nodded her head. "I think so, yeah. Just don't tell Lorraine. I don't think she'd be too happy."

—

Lorraine gasped.

Chris pushed her back against the wall, showing little in the way of consideration for her personal well-being. But that was okay; she liked it rough sometimes, especially when she was drunk. After a few drinks, her inhibitions would always melt away. She was a freak then, and Chris fucking loved it.

They were outside. They'd found a quiet spot to the side of the building. There was nobody around, no prying eyes to watch them as they fucked. Not that Lorraine would've minded that too much either. She found the thought of somebody watching her to be a real turn on.

Chris kissed her deeply, his tongue probing her mouth. Lorraine stroked his tongue with her own. His hands were already under her dress, sliding up the length of her thighs, lifting her skirt, until they found the elastic of her panties.

Lorraine reached forward and stroked Chris' dick through his jeans. He was already erect. Quickly, she unzipped his flies and released his rock-hard member into the open air, her hand wrapped tightly around it, stroking back and forth.

Chris worked Lorraine's underwear to one side, sliding his fingers into her moist slit.

Lorraine moaned, a warm pleasure coursing through her body. She pulled Chris in close, lifting her right leg, and tilting her pelvis, giving him full access. Chris lined the head of his cock with the opening to her vagina, then thrust his hips forward.

Lorraine moaned as Chris began to fuck her. "Yes baby!" she whimpered, gasping between each thrust of his hips. "That's it! Fuck me! Just like that!"

Chris kissed Lorraine on the neck, nibbling gently at her skin. He squeezed her breasts, kneading the flesh through the thin material of the dirtied, torn dress she was wearing.

Lorraine closed her eyes as her orgasm began to build. She pulled Chris in even closer, grinding her hips against his. "Oh… Fuck… Yes…" Her muscles began to quiver as an intense feeling of ecstasy washed over her. She took a deep breath.

Then she opened her eyes…

There was a man standing there, right behind Chris. He was dressed all in black, some kind of black mask over his face. A Halloween costume, perhaps? Neither of them had heard him approach, not over the sounds of their own passionate lovemaking.

He was holding something in his hands. It was long and narrow. An iron bar, perhaps, or some kind of steel tube. Whatever it was, the end had been twisted and crushed, worked into a sharp point.

Lorraine didn't have time to scream. She could offer Chris no warning. Before she even knew what was happening, the man had driven the spiked end of the bar through Chris' back. It had then continued on, out through his chest, penetrating Lorraine through her own stomach. She felt the steel tear through her spine, impaling her to the wall behind her.

Chris screamed.

Lorraine screamed.

She could feel the blood pouring down her legs. She didn't know whose blood this was though; was it hers, or Chris'? The answer, of course, was that it belonged to the both of them. Blood oozed from the wound in her stomach, and combined with blood leaking from Chris' matching wound.

Chris fell limp almost instantly. It took a few moments longer for the life to escape Lorraine's body. Her eyes rolled back in her head as she took her final breath.

—

Helen and Kevin walked side by side, around the yard. Helen trailed her hand against the corn that surrounded them, allowing her fingers to brush against the stalks, causing the leaves to rattle. They didn't talk much; there wasn't much to talk about. The whole thing made Helen consider whether or not they could even really be friends. Did they even have that much in common? She wasn't sure that they did. Perhaps there had only ever been physical attraction between them.

She found this thought to be somewhat comforting, as she knew that this meant she'd soon get over him.

"Come on," said Kevin. "Shall we get back inside? We're missing the party."

"Yeah, sure," agreed Helen. "The others will probably be wondering where we've gotten too."

"Where *you've* gotten to, more like. I don't think they give a shit about me."

Helen laughed. "Yeah," she said. "That's true!" At least he still had a sense of humour.

Helen hadn't realised it, but they had actually strayed quite far from the slaughterhouse. Looking back, she found that they were actually somewhere near the back of the building. With Kevin taking the lead, they made their way towards the fire escape door at the far corner, knowing that this would take them into the corridor behind the stage.

There, Helen reached for the handle. But before she could pull the door open, Kevin had placed his hand against it, preventing her from doing so.

He was close to her now, closer than she really felt comfortable with. And he was smiling, an almost lecherous look on his face. "So," he said. "Are we okay?"

At first, Helen didn't really know what he meant, nor did she understand why he was suddenly acting like such a creep. Then again, perhaps he wasn't; perhaps it was just her drunken mind playing tricks on her. "Yeah," she said, the annoyance audible in her voice. "We're fine."

"And are you sure there's nothing that can happen between us?"

"Yes. I'm sure."

He placed a hand on her shoulder, a touch that she hadn't invited, nor did she want. Something about Kevin's demeanour had changed, like he wasn't about to take no for an answer. "Are you sure I can't make it up to you?"

"No," said Helen, shrugging his hand away from her shoulder. "You can't. And, you know what? I don't think I'd *want* you to. I don't think I even know who you are anymore." She turned and marched away, towards the back of the slaughterhouse.

Behind her, she heard Kevin groan. He was following her then, calling after her. "Come on, Helen!" he called. "I was just messing around! You don't need to be like this!"

Helen turned the corner of the building. Suddenly, she froze. Her eyes widened, her breath catching in her lungs.

Kevin turned the corner behind her. Like Helen, he too froze.

"Oh my God!" muttered Helen.

Before her, all piled up into a heap, was what appeared to be five or six corpses, each one slathered with blood, their skin pale.

"What the fuck?" grunted Kevin.

Helen's eyes darted across the human remains before her. There were faces in there that she recognised – Lorraine, and Anna, and Chris. There were others there too, people she didn't recognise.

Helen screamed. Immediately, her breathing became racked with harsh sobs that burned in her chest.

Kevin grabbed her by the top of her arm, pulling her around, dragging her eyes away from the carnage before her. "Come on! We need to get out of here!"

"We need to get help!" Helen insisted. "We need to warn the others!"

"No. We need to get as far away from this place as possible. We'll go the police station, they can send somebody out here."

Helen wasn't thinking. She didn't know if that was the right thing to do or not. Her body seemed to be on autopilot, following Kevin as he pulled her along, across the yard, towards the cars parked there. "Where are we going?" she asked, tears rolling down her cheeks.

"I borrowed my brother's car," Kevin told her, stressing the urgency.

"But… you don't have a license." Helen knew this to be true; Kevin had taken his driving test once before, and had failed.

"Who gives a shit. We need to get out of here. It's already open, get in."

Helen didn't argue any further. Kevin jumped into the driver's seat of the beaten-up Nissan parked amongst the others, while Helen climbed in on the passenger side. Within a few seconds Kevin had fired up the engine and they were speeding away from the slaughterhouse, and onto the country lanes.

She knew they shouldn't have left everybody else behind. Not when there was a killer on the loose.

Fuck...

There was *another* killer. Was that even possible? How? This was totally insane. She had killed Mark herself. He was dead; Helen was sure of it. So this wasn't him. Then who?

Lorraine was dead.

Anna was dead.

Chris was dead, too.

Shit… Was Ryan there in that pile of corpses? She hadn't seen. If he wasn't – if he was still alive somewhere – then they'd just left him behind, at the mercy of this new psychopath.

How was it possible that there was more than one killer? Had Mark been working with somebody else? He must've been; that was the only possible explanation. But then, why? What the fuck was going on? And if there was two of them, was it possible that there was more?

"It's okay," said Kevin. "We're alright now. I'll take us some place safe."

Helen looked at Kevin, her vision blurred by the tears washing over her eyeballs. Where was he taking her? "We need to go to the police. We need to tell them what's happening."

"Yeah. Of course. I know. That's what I meant. The police station is probably the safest place to be right now."

Helen looked around, out through the car windows. The headlights flashed over an infinite expanse of corn, each row taller than the car itself. She couldn't help but wonder if they were heading in the right direction. She didn't recognise this place – why would she? – but she couldn't help but consider whether or not Kevin really knew where he was going.

"Did you see who was there?" Kevin asked, his words rushed, panicked. "Lorraine was dead, wasn't she?"

Helen nodded, almost feeling numb now. "And Anna, and Chris too."

"Fuu*uuccck...*"

Helen could feel her heart racing. Kevin was a good guy. He'd never hurt her. He wasn't the killer. He certainly hadn't killed Lorraine, or Anna – she'd been with him when… whoever it was… when they… But, did he know about it? Was he a psychopath, just like Mark? She hadn't thought *Mark* was capable of killing anybody, and look how wrong she'd been.

Her thoughts trailed back to when Mark had died. He'd said some strange things to her then, things that were seemingly starting to make more sense now. He'd said that it wasn't over. He'd referred to *them*. Had he meant this second killer? '*They're already here'*… That's what he'd said. He hadn't been talking about one person; he was a talking about many.

Was he talking about Kevin?

Helen looked to Kevin once more.

Something caught the corner of her eye – a shape behind her, in the back seat.

A man, dressed in black, just like Mark had been on that fateful night.

Helen screamed.

"Holy fuck!" yelled Kevin, having looked into the rear-view mirror, to see the man now seated behind him. He pulled down on the steering wheel, causing the car to swerve, tyres skidding along the road.

The man in the mask dove forward. He was holding a knife. He grabbed Kevin around the face, and plunged the blade into the side of his neck.

Helen was still screaming.

Blood squirted from the wound in the side of Kevin's throat, coating the inside of the windscreen in gore. The killer tore the knife free, then plunged it back in, over and over. He must've stabbed Kevin more than a dozen times, a huge gash opening up in his neck.

Kevin was dead, and the car was out of control. It careened from the road, scraping across the uneven edge of the tarmac. It hit the ditch beside the road, then spun, the tyres digging into the wet mud. Then the car flipped. A deafening noise filled the vehicle; the crunch of twisted metal, the squeal of steel on tarmac.

Helen was thrown to one side, then to the other. She saw the killer slam into the roof of the car, saw the knife tumble from his grip. She closed her eyes and held her breath, waiting for the world to stop spinning.

Moments later, everything fell still.

With pain coursing through every one of her limbs, like rusted nails had been driven into each joint, Helen dragged herself out of the wrecked car, only looking back for a single second, to see that Kevin was truly dead.

He was. He was upside down, pinned to his seat by the belt she hadn't even notice him putting on. Blood still pumped from his savaged neck, the ichor pouring down his face.

The killer was there too. He seemed dazed, but he was still alive.

She needed to get out of there.

She pushed herself up to her feet, and ran, cutting off the road and into the field of corn.

--- --- --- --- --- --- --- --- --- --- --- ---

There must be a thousand different ways to kill somebody. Of course, I don't really kill anybody. What I do is make-believe. But if I really wanted to kill somebody, I'm sure I could come up with some creative ways to do so. There are so many places to look for inspiration, so many great films filled with iconic deaths. Who could forget the meat-hook impalement from Texas Chainsaw Massacre*? It wouldn't surprise me to find that murderers took inspiration from these movies. But that doesn't mean that these movies are responsible for their psychotic tendencies.*

Adam Chambers, independent

filmmaker and horror movie fanatic

Chapter Twelve:

Wrong Way

Helen could still see the image of Kevin's body, hanging upside down in the car, his safety belt pinning him into his inverted seat, the blood pouring down his face in torrents, saturating his hair, dripping onto the roof below, and soaking the fabric liner black. It was as if this picture had been burned into her retinas. It was something she knew she wouldn't soon forget – if she ever forgot it at all.

But then, she wasn't sure she *wanted* to forget. Kevin was dead. He had been brutally murdered, and she had done nothing to try and stop it. No – it was stupid for her to think that way; there was nothing she possibly could've done. But still, perhaps she didn't *deserve* to forget that image. Perhaps she deserved to be haunted by that image for the rest of her miserable life.

And just how short might that life be? The killer was still alive. It seemed entirely likely that he – assuming it *was* a he – would have escaped the wrecked car by now, and would soon be giving chase.

Helen's feet squelched through the soft mud, feeling as if she were sinking down to her ankles, the white Reeboks she'd worn beneath her Halloween costume undoubtedly ruined already, the dress itself spattered brown. She was surrounded on all sides by rows of corn, stretching on endlessly in all directions, obscuring her vision, and flipping her sense of direction on its head. She should've stuck to the road. At least then she'd have known where exactly she was headed. But then again, that would mean that the killer too would know where she was going. They'd have caught her with ease, surely. Then she'd be dead.

No – leaving the road and heading into the corn had to be the best option. She was hidden there. There was no possible way that the killer could've seen her. Unless, of course, they were taller than the corn. But the corn had to be at least six feet tall. It was way above Helen's head. It had to be over the head of *most* people. But if the killer did just so happen to be taller than the corn, then they might be able to see the ears of corn being brushed aside as Helen pushed through.

And what about her footprints? Would the killer be able to follow *them*? It seemed unlikely; although the sky was clear, the moonlight failed to penetrate the corn, doing little to illuminate the ground beneath her feet.

Why was he doing this? The killer – it had to be a man, right? – had been waiting for them in the back of Kevin's car. That meant he'd specifically targeted them. He wanted them dead. Why? What had they done to deserve this? Had they hurt him in some way? And what about Anna and Lorraine? What was it that *they* had done?

What had any of them done?

Then there was Kevin. Sure, they weren't together anymore. They hadn't been for some time. Helen didn't love him anymore, she was sure of that. But she still cared for him. She wouldn't have ever wanted to see him hurt in such a way. And she'd just left him there…

But what else could she have done? She couldn't have known that the killer was there, waiting for them in the back seat of the car. The truth was, she was lucky to be alive herself. And then, it wasn't as if she could've pulled his corpse from the car and taken it with her, was it? The killer was still out there. As far as Helen was concerned, she was still his intended victim. She might as well have had a target painted on her back.

Fuck. Where was she going? She couldn't keep running forever. She needed to formulate a plan. Would there be any farmhouses out here, perhaps? These corn fields couldn't go on forever, surely. They had to end at some point, and then Helen would find herself. Well… she'd at least know where she was. Then she could look for help.

Maybe she should head back to the road. Maybe heading into the corn was a stupid idea after all. At least on the road, she might chance upon somebody driving by. She could flag them down, get them to help her. But heading back to the road now was almost an impossibility; she had no idea as to which direction the road now was.

Yet, perhaps some random stranger driving along the road might still be her salvation. They'd see Kevin's crashed car, right? They find him inside, his throat cut wide open. They'd fetch help. Hopefully, it wouldn't be too late by then.

Helen continued to run, the corn whipping her as she crossed the field. It was only then that she became painfully aware of the sound. She hadn't noticed it before, what with her being fixated on running as fast as her legs might go, but as she pushed each stalk aside, she found that the leaves rattled noisily. She'd worried the killer might be able to see the corn moving as she passed through. But that would be entirely unnecessary; in all likelihood, they'd be able to *hear* her.

This thought took a grip of her heart and squeezed, panic starting to fill her lungs, like a liquid drowning her. Fuck. What if the killer was right behind her?

She had to keep going. Just keep running.

Helen couldn't help but think about her mother. She wished she were there with her. She'd know what to do, having fought off and killed a psychotic murderer before. That was the one thing that Helen and her mother now had in common. Just like Helen herself, her mother was a survivor. She… she…

At college, they'd joked that maybe *she* was the killer. They'd said that maybe she'd gone crazy, what with it being the anniversary of that massacre all those years ago. But that just wasn't possible, was it? An odd feeling of doubt began to creep into Helen's bones. It was foolish, she knew that. She was just being paranoid. Her mother wasn't a killer. She wasn't insane. What possible reason could she have for wanting to kill Helen and her friends? To Helen's mind, it was more likely to be George Milton himself, back from the dead, a vengeful bloodlust driving him to kill.

Shit – that sounded like the plot to one of those stupid video nasties…

The police had accused Russ of the murders. They had arrested him, but then they'd released him soon after. It wasn't him; he'd become one of Mark's victims himself.

Helen thought about Mark and the things he'd done. She could still feel his weak grip around her throat, his blood leaking from the wound in his chest – the wound *she* had inflicted.

Mark was dead, but it seemed clear now that he hadn't been acting alone. Who was it behind this mask? Who was it that had killed Lorraine and Anna and Chris and Kevin? And where was Ryan?

Ryan. It had to be him, didn't it? He and Mark had planned this whole thing together, and now he was finishing the job.

A sudden impact to Helen's shoulder knocked her off her feet, sending her sprawling face down into the sodden dirt, the taste of mud spattering her lips, the wind knocked from her sails. Quickly, she rolled to her back, her heart in her throat.

A giant towered over her, his arms outstretched, his ragged shirt and trousers hanging from his emaciated straw body, his woven hat sitting crooked on top of his head, his blank face staring down at her.

It was a scarecrow. She'd ran into a fucking scarecrow! Thank the Lord!

Better still was the fact that, if there was a scarecrow out here in the field, then that meant there must be a farm nearby. But in which direction? Helen hopped up to her feet and looked all around, trying to see through the rows of corn, hoping that she might see some light, somewhere off in the distance.

But it was no good. She could see nothing but the corn.

But that didn't mean the farm wasn't there. It *had* to be somewhere. She needed to find it. There had to be something to tell her which way she ought to run. She looked to her right – nothing. She looked to her left – nothing. She looked past the scarecrow, along the narrow rows.

A hulking man stood there, little more than a shadow, his shoulders rising and falling rapidly in time with his laboured breaths.

Moonlight glistened from the bloodstained blade of his knife. He swung for Helen.

Helen yelped as she dodged backward, her feet slipping out from under her once more. Back in the mire, she scrambled backward, her palms slipping on the wet ground, failing to gain purchase. But then the man was stalking towards her, causing her actions to become more frantic. She pushed up, and flipped to her front, tucking her knees up to her chest, and driving off her heels.

The man swung for her again, the blade missing by less than an inch.

She was running again, the man following her, his strides long, never even breaking into so much as a jog.

Isn't that what happened in those movies? The killer never ran, did they?

Helen was running though, as fast as she possibly could. She knew she shouldn't look back, but she simply couldn't help herself. The killer was still behind her, matching her almost pace for pace. How was that even possible? Was it that she was just so exhausted that her legs weren't really working the way they *felt* they were, and that she was actually running at a much slower pace than she imagined?

The killer sliced at her once more, the blade catching her this time, the steel tearing through her shoulder with ease, scraping against her scapula, the sudden shock of the impact, along with the instant burning agony that accompanied it, sending her sprawling once again.

Sobbing now, with nowhere to run, Helen rolled to her back and raised her hands, as if she might somehow be able to defend herself. "Please," she begged, her breathing racked, tears streaking down her cheeks. "Don't kill me. Please. Just let me go."

For the first time, she was able to look the killer in the eyes. He was dressed in all black, his head covered with a woollen balaclava. But his eyes were visible, and they belonged to a human.

Of course they did. For the briefest of moments, Helen had imagined herself being confronted by some inhuman monster. But this was no such thing. This was a man.

"Please," Helen begged once more. "Please, just let me go."

The man ignored her pleas. He raised the knife above his head and dropped to his knees, driving the point of the steel downward, towards Helen's face. Helen pulled to one side and lifted her arms to deflect the blow. But she was unsuccessful in doing so; the blade pierced the palm of her left hand, sliding between the metacarpal bones inside.

Helen screamed as the man tore the knife free.

But she had no time to do anything else. Once again, the man was pushing the knife in towards her face, the point just a few millimetres away from puncturing her eyeball. Arms raised, she gritted her teeth and pushed against the man's wrist. She swung her arm, the point of her elbow colliding with his cheekbone, loosening his grip ever so slightly.

Helen clawed at the man's face, attempting to drive her thumbs into his eye sockets. The killer squirmed, twisting his head to one side, causing Helen's thumbs to slam uselessly into his forehead.

The effect this *did* have, however, was to tear the man's balaclava away from his face, her nails catching in the woollen material, sliding it upwards and over his head.

The face that Helen saw before her was one she didn't recognise. This surprised her to no end; for a moment she'd been sure that it was Ryan chasing her through the corn. If not him, then Mark, or George Milton, back from the dead. At the very least, she expected it to be somebody she knew, so that she could understand their reasons for doing this.

But this was a man she felt sure she'd never seen before. He was, perhaps, in his mid-twenties. He had a neatly trimmed beard and perfectly blue eyes. His mid-length hair was tousled from where the balaclava had been pulled free.

Both Helen and the man froze, staring deep into each other's eyes. It was as if they were trying to read each other's mind.

Helen took that moment of peace to strike. She slammed her knee upward, into the man's groin, causing him to recoil, grunting angrily through his gritted teeth.

Helen screamed; an involuntary sound, brought on by her desperate exertion. She wrestled with the man's wrist, twisting it back, wrenching the knife free from his grasp. She kicked out then, her heels pushing deep into his abdomen, forcing him back. Then she was scrambling backward, rolling to her knees, up to her feet.

She turned, the killer already up to his own feet, coming for her now. Helen held the knife out before her. "Stop right there!" she screamed. "Don't come any closer! I *will* kill you!"

The man raised his hands in surrender. "I know you will Helen," he said.

The sound of her own name stunned Helen momentarily. How did this stranger know her name? "Who the fuck are you?" she growled, her voice breaking, her throat horse. "Why are you doing this? What the fuck do you want from me?"

"So many questions," said the man. He took a step towards her. Helen matched it, stepping back. "You don't know who I am?"

Helen shook her head. "Am I *supposed* to know who you are?"

"Some people do, some people don't," he said, shrugging his shoulders. "I guess it depends on who you ask. My name is David Copley. I write for a magazine called Video News Weekly. I write about horror movies."

Helen was confused. That didn't answer any of the multitude of questions that had infested her brain. If anything, it made her understand even *less*. "I don't get. What the fuck is going on? Why do you want to kill me? Why did you kill my friends?"

"Well, I think that's fairly obvious, isn't it?" smirked David. "Mark can't very well be here to do it, can he? Not now that he's – how should I put this? – indisposed."

"You mean he's fucking dead!"

"Indeed."

David took another step toward Helen. Helen matched it, once again. "But why are you doing this *at all*?" Helen asked.

"Perhaps I'm just insane," said David, as if this were the only answer anybody could possibly have needed. But then he added, "Perhaps I've just seen way too many video nasties!"

No. That was ridiculous. No amount of exposure to horror movies could possibly drive someone insane, no matter how violent they were. What all those politicians and campaigners had been saying, it was all nonsense. The films themselves weren't dangerous. They couldn't possibly be.

But then again, perhaps those films were enough to tip a deranged mind over the edge. Somebody who was already on the verge of being psychotic might be inspired to commit their own heinous acts of violence and cruelty by the things they saw in those movies. Was that possible? Not only was it possible, to Helen, it seemed increasingly likely. This guy was insane; *something* had driven him to kill.

And what about Mark? He'd said that he wanted to make his own video nasty. Had the two of them simply been insane? Did they somehow know each other, and had they planned all of this just for their own sick amusement?

No – this was something else, something bigger.

It *had* to be.

"I don't *think* I'm insane, though," David continued. "I'm not sure that there's anything wrong with my brain. It's not like those movies have… have… *broken* me in any way. I just love them, you know? I just love the blood and the terror. They're just so much fun. Maybe that's what I wanted. I just… I wanted to make my own real life video nasty. And get this – you're the star! You're the final girl!"

Helen couldn't believe what she was hearing. "Are you fucking serious?" she said. "You and Mark killed all those people just so you could create your own sick horror movie in your head? And you think you *aren't* insane?"

David shrugged his shoulders once again. "Who knows? But you have to admit, it has been exciting, hasn't it? I'm surprised we both got out of that crash alive! We should probably both be dead right now!"

He was laughing then. This was all just some kind of joke to him. It was a game. It was as if this wasn't even reality he was living in. It was as if he was inside his own twisted little movie.

David took a step towards Helen. "Don't worry though, you will be dead soon. I just need to decide *how* I'm going to do it. We had hoped to kill all our victims in the same way that people died in the nasties. Mark did a respectable job. He drilled through that one girl's skull like in *Driller Killer*, and he killed that punk kid with garden shears, like Cropsey used in *The Burning*. I decapitated that one friend of yours with an axe. That was supposed to be from *Nightmares In A Damaged Brain*."

Helen hadn't seen anybody with their head cut off. Was he talking about Ryan, perhaps? Ryan had left the party to go and smoke a joint, and Helen hadn't seen him since. Was he lying dead somewhere now, with his head removed from his body?

David continued – "Stabbing your little boyfriend to death like that wasn't exactly part of the plan either, but I had to improvise. And now, I can't *for the life of me* think of a way to kill *you*. I had hoped to kill somebody with a pitchfork. That would cover both *Rosemary's Killer* and *The Slayer*. Alas, I don't *actually* have a pitchfork on hand right now, so…"

David sprang forward, knocking the knife out of Helen's hand, thrusting the heel of his palm forcefully into the side of her jaw, dazing her, knocking her off her feet once more.

Breathing heavy, her lungs aching, Helen watched as David scanned the ground for his knife. Seeing that he was distracted, Helen flipped over, and pushed herself up onto her feet. She was running again then, not daring to look back this time.

"Get back here, little girl!" David's voice called through the corn. "It's no good running! I *will* catch you!"

A few moments of running, and Helen saw the corn thinning out before her. That meant she had found her way back to the road. Perhaps now she might be saved. She was going to make it.

She burst from the corn field, onto the road, only to be immediately bathed in the headlights of an oncoming car.

Helen raised her hands instinctively, to shield her eyes from the light, her body now rigid.

The brakes of the car screeched, the machine swerving side to side, as the driver pulled on the wheel. Thankfully, whoever was behind the wheel, they were able to manoeuvre the car around the girl who had seemingly appeared from nowhere before them. Groaning, the car slid along the beaten tarmac.

Helen held her breath. She half expected the car to flip, much like Kevin's had earlier. But this driver had kept control, miraculously able to keep all four wheels on the road, albeit now pointing in the opposite direction.

Helen ran along the road, towards the car. She slammed into the passenger side door, her palms hammering against the window. "Please," she said, frantically. "You have to help me! He's trying to kill me!" And then, as she realised just who it was who had been driving the car, her breath caught in her throat.

"Oh my God."

--- --- --- --- --- --- --- --- --- --- --- ---

It amazes me that people still deem it necessary to question whether 'evil' truly exists. Of course it does! You only need to look around you. Take a look at what your children are reading nowadays, or watching on their televisions. It is nothing short of grotesque. It is filth. And now there are these so-called "video nasties"... Even the titles are wholly inappropriate. Gestapo's Last Orgy… I Spit On Your Grave… Blood Feast… Killer Nun. *What kind of a person would want to watch such movies? And let's not forget films like* Snuff, *and* Faces Of Death, *and* Cannibal Holocaust… *These are movies that actually show real people being murdered in real life! How can we allow such depravity into our homes? It's no wonder these movies are capable of turning good, decent people into demented maniacs.*

Gary Smart, conservative MP and

campaigner against social liberalism

Chapter Thirteen:

Evilspeak

"Oh my God," said Helen, as she pulled open the driver's side door. Her heart hammered the inside of her ribcage, her lungs burning even more so now. "Are you okay?"

Margaret Whitehead was sitting there in the driver's seat, her eyes rolling around in their respective sockets, dazed, as if her brains had been scrambled. "Wh-what… what happened?" And then, as the fog quickly cleared from behind her eyes, the memory of the proceeding thirty seconds returned to her, and she looked to Helen. "Oh, dear God… Are you okay?"

Helen nodded. And then there were tears streaming down her face, the relief building inside and finally overflowing. "I am," she whimpered. "But… there's a man in the corn. He… he was chasing me. He was… was trying to kill me. His name is David… D-David Copley… He's the one who killed everybody!"

Margaret's eyes widened, staring blankly off into the distance. "David Copley? I… I know that name," she said, shaking her head dismissively. "But… no… the murderer is dead."

"Yeah," said Helen. "*I'm* the one who killed him. But this is somebody else. There's another killer!"

"That was *you*?" Margaret shook her head once again, this time as if she were trying to unscramble her thoughts. "Wait. That's right… I passed a car, just a moment ago. It was on its roof. I stopped to help, but, the boy in the driver's seat – he was dead."

"I was in that car," Helen said, nodding her head. "And so was the killer. He… he killed the driver, and caused the car to crash."

"Oh, dear…" Margaret was frowning. She looked back to Helen. "Why would he do that?"

"I don't know," Helen sobbed. "But he did! And then he chased me through that field."

"But you got away?"

Helen nodded once again. Suddenly then, it occurred to her that Margaret didn't trust her. She'd seen Margaret before, but never so close, never so that they might be able to speak. But now she could look her over more closely, she could see that Margaret was quite frail. Her eyes were ringed in grey, and her skin was sallow, hanging from her bones in thick, wrinkled folds. As she spoke, her chapped lips seemed to peel away from her gums. Her curled hair, completely white, was thinning to the point that her scalp was visible. And as she peered over her glasses, there was an obvious look of uncertainty in her eyes.

"He nearly caught me," said Helen, confirming that she had escaped. "But I kicked him in the balls and I ran."

Margaret nodded, understanding. She took a breath. "Come on, dear," she said. "Get in. I think we ought to get out of here."

Helen didn't bother to check her surroundings. There was no way that David could get to her, not now, not before she got into the car. She was safe. She was going to make it. Quickly, she closed the driver's side door, then ran around the car, before jumping into the passenger seat.

The car had stalled when Margaret had slammed on the brakes, to prevent herself from splattering Helen on the tarmac. Margaret turned the key in the ignition. The engine turned over, but failed to fire.

A sense of despair punched Helen in the gut, her heart skipping a beat or two. For a moment, she assumed that the car wasn't going to start, that they were going to have to get out and walk. And what good would this old lady be when it came to fighting off a serial killer? It wasn't as if David was a small guy either, but that was the least of her concerns. The fact remained that he had a knife, and he was more than willing to slice through flesh with it. "What's wrong?" said Helen, her voice wavering. "Why won't it start?"

"It's an old car," said Margaret. "It just takes a few goes sometimes."

Sure enough, within a few tries, the engine had started, and they were off along the road, the path carved through the stalks of corn leading the way.

"The man who attacked you," Margaret asked. "You said his name was David Copley? I know him. He writes for a magazine. He's a vehement opposer of mine."

Was that why he was doing this? Was it something to do with Margaret and her campaign against the video nasties? Regardless, Helen offered no response.

"What were you doing out here anyway?" Margaret asked nonchalantly, as if they were simply having a pleasant conversation as they drove.

Helen didn't really feel like talking. She was more concerned about surviving. But Margaret was looking at her from the corner of her eye, waiting for an answer. And Margaret had possibly saved her life, so it only seemed fair for Helen to answer. "I was at a party," she said. "At the old slaughterhouse. David, he… I found a bunch of bodies there. He killed my friends!"

"What kind of a party takes place in a slaughterhouse?" Margaret scoffed, almost dismissing the part about the dead bodies. "That sounds a little morbid to me."

Helen shook her head, knowing how stupid it sounded. "It was a Halloween party. It was *supposed* to be morbid."

Margaret tutted. "I'll never understand you kids, dressing up, and partying in a slaughterhouse, watching these grotesque horror films. I just don't get it."

"No. I know you don't."

Margaret looked at Helen, her eyebrows raised once more. "Oh. So you *do* know who I am?"

"Of course. I've seen you on TV. I saw you the other day in town actually, outside the video shop, after Mark… the original killer. After I killed him. You were there, talking about how dangerous these films are."

"Yes, dear. And it seems I was correct."

Helen couldn't disagree, not after everything David had said to her in the corn. Mark had said the same thing. She still didn't understand it, but that was what this was, he'd said so himself; he wanted to make his own video nasty.

"The police arrested that boy," Margaret said, referring to Russ. "They may have let him go, and I know he's dead now, but I still think he was involved somehow."

Helen turned in her seat. She shook her head. "No. Mark was the original killer. I killed him. But now there's David. I don't even know who he is, but he tried to kill me too. He and Mark must've known each other somehow."

"Yes," said Margaret. "So maybe that boy from the video shop was working with them too."

Helen scoffed, her distain for this woman already beginning to grow. "No. I knew him. He wasn't a murderer. And I don't see what the fuck that matters now anyway."

Margaret glared at Helen, a deep anger in her grey eyes. For just a moment, Helen seemed to sense a feeling of hatred emanating from her. But then it was gone, her facial features softening. "I'm sorry, dear," Margaret said. "I just don't know *what* to believe right now."

Helen sighed, slumping back in her seat.

There, in the distance, along the road, was Kevin's overturned car. Smoke was billowing from the underside of the engine bay now, a small fire having started somewhere inside. Margaret slowed the car as they passed, once again looking in. Helen didn't look. She didn't need to see what was inside. She didn't want to see Kevin's corpse again, didn't need to see his blood-soaked face.

Once they had passed the car, and they were once again cruising along the road, Helen looked across to Margaret. "There was a scarecrow out in the field," she said. "There must be a farmhouse out here somewhere. We should find it, and call the police."

"That's exactly where we're headed, my dear," nodded Margaret. "I know where that farmhouse is."

At least that was something.

After a moment of silence, Margaret spoke once again. "Tell me, dear," she said, her eyes remaining fixed on the road ahead, "you're the girl who killed the murderer, yes? The first one, I mean."

"Yes."

"So, you're also the girl whose mother survived that massacre here, back in nineteen-sixty-two, yes?"

What a bizarre question. How could this woman possibly know that? And why would she even be asking? Instead of answering, Helen's brain told her that, for some reason, she needed to try and stall this line of questioning. "Wh… what?" she stammered.

"There was a massacre here, back in nineteen-sixty-two, I believe it was. From what I understand, that also took place at a Halloween party. Many people died. But there was one girl who survived. Somebody told me that this was your mother."

Helen felt as if she were choking. "Who told you that?"

Margaret didn't answer. She just looked at Helen out of the corner of her eye, then turned her attention back to the road. "For years now," she said. "I've tried to help people understand just how dangerous the media is, that the media — in particular, these so-called video nasties —are turning our society into a population of braindead monsters. But the truth is, these monsters have existed forever, haven't they? George Milton murdered all those people more than twenty years ago now. I don't think he ever watched *The Last House On The Left*, did he?"

Helen was looking at Margaret, staring daggers into her. Who did this woman think she was? Why was she bringing this up now? And how did she know it was her mother who had been the sole survivor of Milton's rampage?

Margaret continued, "People are fallible creatures. The intelligence that God has bestowed upon us is really a curse. Our brains need constant stimulation. We need something to occupy our minds, or else they revert to the more savage thoughts that plague all wild animals. Anybody could become a psychopath, given the right circumstances."

Was she talking about *her*? Was she implying that Helen herself might be psychotic?

"Video nasties," Margaret went on. "They are just one small part of the puzzle. Sex and drugs are also key factors. It's no surprise that this friend of yours — the boy you killed — might've been driven crazy. This is exactly the sort of thing I've been talking about. And now there's *another* killer? Perhaps they weren't related at all. Perhaps they were *both* just corrupted by the media."

Helen considered this momentarily. David had said he was a writer – something that Margaret herself had confirmed. He said he wrote about horror movies, said he wanted to make his own video nasty. That was the exact same thing that Mark had said. Maybe Margaret was right after all.

"And yet," Margaret continued, "still, we have people like George Milton. I'm sure sex and drugs played a part in the crimes he committed too, but still, I always wonder if there's something else we've been missing."

"What?" scoffed Helen, a fury bubbling away in the pit of her stomach. She didn't know why she was so angry. Why was this crazy old bitch bringing up the past like this? "Like the fact that he was *fucking* insane?"

Margaret's head snapped across to Helen, and stayed there for more than a few moments, long enough to make her feel uncomfortable, long enough to make her wonder just how the car had managed to remain on the road. "I'll ask you not to talk to me that way, if you don't mind," she said, returning her eyes to the road. "I don't like such foul language".

Helen said nothing. She stared out through the windscreen, the headlights of the car flashing across the corn.

"But, yes, perhaps he *was* simply insane," said Margaret. "Perhaps he was born evil. Is that what your mother saw when she looked into his eyes? Did she see the devil inside him?"

Helen could feel her cheeks flushing. She'd just nearly died at the hands of a serial killer — for the second time, no less — and now this woman was talking to her about the psychopath who tried to murder her mother over twenty years ago. And still, the question remained – how did this woman even know who she was?

Helen was about to ask, but before she could speak, Margaret nodded her head, pointing out the front window with her chin. "Ah," she said. "Here we are."

She was right. A turning, just ahead on the right, cut through the corn, onto a dirt track. Here, the vegetation had been chopped down to a more manageable height, a height that Helen could now see over. Ahead, the farmhouse stood, silhouetted against the purple sky, lights on in some of the rooms. Thank God! That meant that somebody was home. Somebody was there who could help them. They could phone the police… if they had a phone, of course. They *had* to have a phone; everybody had one nowadays. Of course they'd have one. It was their only hope.

Margaret drove the car along the dirt driveway, towards the house. As they neared, Helen tried to look in through the windows, searching for movement, searching for whoever might be inside. But there was nothing; no shadows, no twitching curtains.

Please God, let there be somebody home!

She saw somebody then. A man. He was waiting on the porch, next to the front door, a jack-o'-lantern by his feet on the doorstep, the candle inside flickering in the breeze. As the car approached, he stepped down from the wooden deck to the dirt that surrounded the property, waving his hands above his head as of he'd been expecting them.

The man must've been in his late fifties, or early sixties. His beard and hair were both the purest shade of white. His back seemed to be slightly hunched, and his belly was somewhat distended, both of which were to be expected in a man of his age. He wore a flannel shirt and corduroy trousers. No doubt, this was the owner of the house; he looked very much like a farmer. He was smiling kindly.

"Do you know him?" Helen asked Margaret, her voice barely any more than a whisper.

Margaret slowed the car, and parked it at the front of the house. The farmer lumbered across to the car and pulled open the passenger side door, right next to Helen. He tipped his head, looking past Helen, to Margaret. "Is this her?" he asked.

Margaret nodded. "Yes," she said. "This is her."

The farmer looked into Helen's eyes and smiled. And then he grabbed her, one hand around her throat, the other entangled in a mass of her hair.

Helen screamed as the farmer dragged her out of the car, dumping her unceremoniously onto the hard dirt floor. She landed awkwardly, her arms twisting under her body as she hit the ground face first.

"Careful with her," said Margaret, as she herself climbed out of the car. "We don't want to hurt her. Not yet, anyway."

The air had been knocked from Helen's lungs. Her brain was pulsating, pushing painfully against the backs of her eyes. *What the fuck is going on?* Helen didn't understand. None of this made any sense. Who were these people? Why were they doing this to her. Margaret Whitehead was supposed to be a good woman. A God-fearing woman. Why would she have brought Helen here, to this vile man who had, only seconds ago, roughly dragged her from the car? Were they going to kill her? Mark had tried to kill her, and so had David. Between them, they'd killed all her friends. Clearly, they were somehow connected. But was Margaret involved too? And the farmer?

And then she saw *him*.

The killer – David Copley – was standing there, having emerged from around the corner of the house. He was still dressed all in black, although he had now discarded the balaclava. The light from inside the house reflected from the dirtied blade of his knife. "I told you I'd catch you," he smirked, his grin stretching from ear to ear.

"Please…" moaned Helen, her ribs burning as she spoke. "What do you want from me?"

Margaret, David and the farmer all stood before her, towering over her crumpled frame. None of them answered her question.

"Please don't do this," Helen begged, desperation dripping from every syllable. "You can't kill me. Please."

"I'm sorry, dear," said Margaret, her voice soft and gentle, almost kindly, yet tinged with a sinister aura. "But this is the way it must be."

Helen hadn't realised it, but tears were now streaming down her face, washing the dirt from her cheeks. She was breathing heavy, fear invading her lungs, her body growing weaker by the second. It was over. She was dead. There was no point in trying to fight it anymore.

"Is everybody here?" Margaret asked the farmer.

"Yes," said the farmer. "Everybody's inside."

"Good." Margaret turned to David then, and said, "Help her up, will you?"

"But I'm not done playing with her," David said through gritted teeth. "I want to watch her bleed."

"I think you've tormented this poor girl enough. Let's just get her inside, shall we?"

"Okay. Fine." David sounded like a sulky teenager, rather than the grown adult he was supposed to be. Maybe that was a symptom of being a psychopath. "Whatever."

Obediently, David grabbed Helen beneath her armpits and hoisted her from the ground, dragging her up the farmhouse porch steps, past the grinning, hollowed-out pumpkin, and into the house. Along the hallway and into the lounge, Helen found herself surrounded by a dozen people – men and women, young and old. They all just looked like ordinary people, all smiling, staring at her. Any one of them could've been a doctor or a teacher or a plumber, or God only knows what else.

David dumped Helen onto the floor in the middle of the sitting room. The room itself was fairly rustic looking; a pair of ancient looking sofas, upholstered in worn leather; a heavy looking bookcase and sideboard, presumably made from oak; an intricately carved mantlepiece, surrounding the fireplace, a small fire burning within. She looked around at the smiling faces, all now staring in her direction.

There was a man, with white hair and thick-lensed glasses, must've been in his fifties. There was a woman, with a blonde perm and hoop earrings, perhaps in her mid-thirties. There was another woman, short, carrying a little extra weight, around sixty, perhaps. There was a black man, tall, shaved head, thick handlebar moustache. A young couple stood side by side, hand in hand, both must've been in their early twenties.

And amongst them were two faces that Helen recognised – a man and a woman, both in their late forties. They were Mark's parents.

"So," said David, turning to Margaret as she followed him into the room. "What now?"

"Now?" said Margaret. "Now we can begin."

Helen pushed herself up into a sitting position. "Begin what?" she said, sniffing back her tears. "Please… why are you doing this? I don't understand."

Margaret smiled. Her teeth were slightly yellowed, but they were perfectly straight, making Helen think that these weren't actually her real teeth. "My dear," she said, in an almost mocking, patronising way, "I wouldn't expect you to understand."

Helen sobbed once, snorting back the snot that filled her nostrils. "Tell me then. Help me understand. What's this got to do with George Milton?"

Margaret shook her head, scoffing a laugh. "This has *nothing* to do with George Milton."

"Then why were you asking me about him? Why were you asking me about my mother."

Margaret smiled again. "I was simply making conversation, dear. I do find the man to be quite interesting. Very unique. His story is quite grotesque."

Helen could feel her body shaking. Exhaustion penetrated every fibre of every muscle. She shook her head. "If this has nothing to do with Milton, then what *is* this about?" She looked to David and asked – "Why did you kill everybody?"

Before David could answer, Margaret interjected. "*He* killed all those people because *I* asked him to."

Helen pulled a deep breath into her lungs. "But… why?" She felt as if she'd asked the same question a hundred times already. She considered the fact that she might never be graced with an answer.

But then Margaret explained it to her. "David here, and Mark, before him, they killed all those people because I asked them to, so that, together, we might bring about the end of days."

Helen didn't understand. *The end of days?* This was insane.

Margaret continued, "I chose this place because of its rather disturbing history. The actions of George Milton are still raw in the minds of many. The blood of his victims still saturates the very soil of this town. Evil already exists here. Another killing spree would only serve to spread fear far and wide."

Helen shook her head, still none the wiser. "I don't get what you're saying. Why would you want that?"

Margaret shook her head, as if the answer should have been entirely obvious. "For the same reason I want as many people as possible watching the video nasties."

Helen looked to the ground, as if she might somehow find an answer beneath her feet. She just didn't understand any of it. What did she mean? Hadn't she tried to *stop* people from watching them? "Why would you want people to watch the video nasties?" Helen asked, the whole idea seeming all the more ridiculous. "You were trying to get them banned."

Margaret chuckled, as if she'd just been told a highly amusing joke. "And what did that serve to do? Has it stopped anybody from watching them? No, it has not. More people know of them now, than they ever would have without my campaign to get them banned. More people have watched them, just as I had planned. And now, with a serial killer on the loose — killing his victims in ways seemingly *inspired by* the video nasties — public outrage is at an all-time high. *Everybody* is talking about them. *Everybody* is watching them. That's exactly what I wanted."

"But…" stuttered Helen, trying to assemble the pieces of the puzzle in her mind. "Why do you *want* people to watch them?"

"That, my dear, is very simple." Margaret was smiling. If it weren't for the crazy shit spewing from her mouth, Helen might've believed her to be the same kindly old woman she'd seen on the TV. "The video nasties are evil, and evil is like an infection. It spreads like a virus. And then it grows. It expands, until it swallows everything whole. And then, when evil consumes the world, our Lord Satan will rise again!"

No.

No, no, no, no, no.

Nope.

Satan? This was fucking crazy. Insane. Ludicrous. This woman couldn't possibly be serious. "What the fuck are you talking about?" said Helen, swallowing back a wad of phlegm, unable to prevent the tears from once again rolling down her cheeks.

"Death and destruction are all we know," said Margaret. "Humanity has caused nothing but suffering. We need Satan to emerge from Hell, to cleanse the Earth, and save us all. Television and home video have only served to rot the minds and the souls of those who gluttonously consume such media. They are dead already. Humanity is dead already. Evil grows; we must not try to stop it. We must embrace it. We must submit to it. We must submit to Satan."

Helen's breath caught in the back of her throat. She couldn't believe what she was hearing. This woman had planned these murders, just so more people would watch video nasties? Just so they would become *more evil*. Surely not. It was crazy to even think such a thing might be possible! Helen shook her head. "You're fucking insane!"

"Oh, I'm afraid not, my dear. Satan is coming. We must be prepared."

Margaret nodded to David. He approached one of the other men in the crowd – the followers, Helen was already considering them, each of them a member of Margaret Whitehead's fucked up satanic cult – and spoke with him, their voices hushed.

Helen considered the fact that she should run. Just get up and sprint, straight out of the house, and into the corn, don't stop, don't look back, just keep going. But she couldn't run. She wouldn't get far. Her body was too exhausted to even stand. Trying to escape this place would be futile.

She closed her eyes and breathed.

Only the sound of the chainsaw prevented her from drifting off into an endless slumber.

Helen opened her eyes. The man in the crowd had handed David the heavy-looking power tool. He was standing before her now, the petrol engine of the chainsaw sputtering, coughing noxious fumes into the atmosphere. He pulled the trigger, revving it, the chain whirring noisily as the jagged steel teeth chewed through air, just a few inches away from Helen's face. "*The Texas Chainsaw Massacre*," said David, staring into her eyes. His eyes looked almost black. Perhaps there really was something evil lurking inside him after all. "It's one of the best video nasties there is, even though there's not really that much gore in it. It's more about what you don't see, you know? I really wanted to kill somebody with a chainsaw, but I never got the chance. Just imagine the mess it would make!"

The excitement in David's voice set Helen's nerves on edge. He sounded so enthusiastic. It sickened her to her stomach, the thought of David laughing as the saw ripped through her flesh and tore through her bones…

Margaret stepped forward. "Okay, David," she said, "that's enough. We don't need to frighten her any more than she already is. It's time we got started."

"Started with what?" said Helen, drawing the old woman's attention.

A demented smile formed on Margaret's face, the creases of her wrinkled cheeks morphing into cavernous valleys. "The ritual, of course."

--- --- --- --- --- --- --- --- --- --- --- ---

The human mind is a powerful thing. But it can also be warped and moulded, just like Play-Doh. Some people are experts in mind manipulation. Oftentimes, journalists (not including yours truly) want their readers to believe the story they are being told, no matter how fantastical it may seem. Take for instance this whole moral panic surrounding the "video nasties" – it is nothing but a thinly veiled lie, designed to manipulate the way people think. These movies, although they are incredibly violent, cannot cause people to become psychotic. Perhaps people are born evil, but, to my mind, what seems more likely is that people become indoctrinated into a certain way of thinking. They are told what to believe, and they are told it in such a way that they don't even question it. That's how cults work. And do you know who the biggest cult in this country is? It's the British government.

David Copley, entertainment journalist

and writer for 'Video News Weekly'

CHAPTER FOURTEEN:

BLOOD RITES

"The resurrection of Satan is almost upon us," said Margaret, addressing the group of followers who surrounded her. They watched her in awe, eyes wide as if she was some great leader. "We must all play our part, if we are to bring about the end of days."

Helen, still on her knees, looked up at the deranged woman. She was insane; she had to be. Nobody in their right mind could believe any of this.

David delicately handed the chainsaw over to Margaret, ensuring that the blade remained between them, pointing away – pointing towards Helen – the entire time.

Margaret seemed to be struggling with the weight of the machine she now held in her hands. It was a cumbersome tool in the hands of most, but in the frail hands of this elderly lady, it looked like it was almost too much to take.

But Margaret steadied herself. She composed herself. She stood before Helen, the engine of the chainsaw rattling as it continued to turn over. David moved around Helen, standing directly behind her, his hands resting gently on her shoulders.

There was nowhere for Helen to go. There could be no escape. Margaret was going to kill her. She was going to chop her into tiny pieces with the saw.

Helen closed her eyes once again. She considered praying to God, begging for his mercy. But she didn't believe in God. She didn't believe in Satan. This whole thing was insane. And there would be no mercy.

"You have served us well…" said Margaret, her voice raised, a powerful sense of determination swelling with her words. "You will have a seat at the Lord's table, I can assure you of this."

Margaret pulled the trigger of the chainsaw, the engine roaring to life as the chain began to spin.

Helen sobbed. Her breath caught in the back of her throat. She squeezed her eyes tight as she waited for the pain to begin.

And then…

"Thank you," said David.

Helen opened her eyes.

Margaret was driving the chainsaw forward. But not for her, not for Helen. She was directing the chainsaw toward David, and he was doing nothing to try and stop it. It was as if he were accepting of it, inviting it in, willing this to happen.

Helen tipped her head back and watched as the blade chewed through David's neck, slicing through the meat and tendons, then crunching through the vertebrae. Blood gushed from his lacerated arteries, the pressure in his veins forcing it out like a fountain. There was a hissing – more a whistle, perhaps – as the chain slurped at the fluids pulsing from his body, the last of the air escaping his lungs.

The blood cascaded, flung in all directions by the saw. It poured over Helen's face, soaking her hair, adhering it to her skin, sticky like tar. She could taste it, bitter and coppery, slipping over her lips and onto her tongue, down into her throat, choking her. The white material of her Halloween costume was instantly stained a deep shade of crimson.

Finally, David's head was severed. It tumbled to the ground, splattering into the puddle in which Helen now knelt.

Margaret released the trigger. The chainsaw's motor stopped rumbling, but she allowed it to continue turning over, coughing and spluttering. She then heaved, and lifted it over her head, her teeth gritted. "Hail Satan!" she said.

"Hail Satan!" echoed the followers.

"My children!" said Margaret, turning on the spot, addressing the people surrounding them now. "Draw closer! The time is upon us! The master awaits! The seeds of evil have been sowed. Hearts have been blackened. The fear that festers inside this one," –she motioned towards Helen– "is all we need to ensure the success of His rebirth."

But Helen didn't feel *fear*. She wasn't *scared*. She felt disgusted and appalled, yes. But fear? No, it wasn't fear that quickened her heart and sickened her stomach. All the terror had drained from her. Now, she simply felt exhausted. She felt numb. She felt as if the world had come crashing down around her. She felt as if her life was already over. Perhaps that was why she was no longer scared; what do the dead have left to fear?

But it wasn't as if she could tell that to these people, was it? Instead, she watched, drenched in gore, as they slowly began their approach, the circle they had formed around her closing in.

Margaret moved around behind Helen. The chainsaw continued to splutter. "Do not fret, my dear," she said, crouching a little so that she could speak directly into Helen's ear. "I'm not going to kill you. You have a far more important purpose now."

Helen blinked slowly, barely even having the energy to do that. She looked to Margaret, to find that she was smiling. She looked like a friendly grandmother, perhaps a little overbearing, but with the best of intentions at heart. That was the image that Margaret had always put across in her television interviews, but Helen knew differently now. She knew that this old lady was utterly insane. She knew that she was psychotic. She knew that she was dangerous.

"Wh-what d-do you want f-from me?" Helen asked, her voice soft. She wasn't even sure she'd said it, not until Margaret offered a response.

Margaret was still smiling. "You'll see."

She was pulling the trigger of the chainsaw then, the blade roaring to life once again, a grey smoke spewing from the exhaust of the motor. She then lowered the saw, carving through David's carcass, chewing through his shoulders and his hips, until the joints split and the limp limbs were separated from the body.

Helen didn't move. She didn't flinch. Even as the blood sprayed from the dismembered corpse, she didn't even look away. She'd seen so much violence, she almost felt numb to it.

The saw continued to hack through flesh and bone, tearing threads from the carpet, as it clipped the living room floor, splintering the floorboards beneath. Margaret cut the hands from the severed arms, and the feet from the legs. And then she cut the arms in half at the elbows, and the legs in half at the knees. She then split the torso in two, across the stomach, allowing the innards to spill from the decimated chest cavity.

The followers, closer now, watched in silent awe as Margaret split the body into more than a dozen pieces. She turned to one of the men then. "Would you be so kind as to help me?" she asked him.

Obediently, the man stepped forward.

"Pick up the head."

The man didn't hesitate. He picked up David's severed head.

"That's it," said Margaret. "Hold it out for me. And hold it steady. We don't want any accidents, do we?"

The man held the head with both hands, one on either side of the face. He held it out at arm's length, directly before him.

Margaret lowered the thundering chainsaw down onto the top of the decapitated head. Blood gushed as the skin tore from the forehead, the scalp peeling away. The bone split easily, as Margaret bisected the skull, right down the middle. Liquefied brain matter leaked out, splashing sporadically as the chain did its thing. When the chainsaw finally made it all the way through, the man released his grip on the two halves and allowed them to drop to the ground.

Margaret finally killed the chainsaw.

Helen was shaking, exhausted. She needed all of this to be over.

But her ordeal was far from over.

Margaret dropped the chainsaw. Helen then watched, horrified, as Margaret began to pile the pieces of David's ravaged corpse into a grotesque mound in the middle of the living room floor. Finally done, she stood back. "Brothers and sisters," she said, once again addressing the followers. "It is time. Satan awaits! Now we must all offer ourselves unto him."

Margaret began to undress, her blood-slicked fingertips working at the plastic buttons of her cardigan. She removed the cardigan and tossed it aside. She then began to work on her blouse.

A wave of confusion swept over Helen. Everything that had happened… Everything that was happening right now… It was all just so bizarre. The followers had all begun to undress, removing their jackets and shrugging them from their shoulders, stepping out of their crumpled trousers and skirts. They were all naked, not a single stitch of clothing between them.

Helen watched as Margaret stripped out of her underwear. Her soft, sagging breasts rested against her stomach, the skin withered and wrinkled. Her crotch was a matt of thin white pubic hair, curled much like the hair on her head. She stood behind Helen, her hands on her shoulders, pulling her back against the soft flesh of her belly. "Come now!" she told the crowd. "Come forth and give yourself to Him!"

Helen's teeth began to chatter. She'd been lying to herself. She wasn't scared – she was terrified. More so now that she had seen the knife that Margaret was holding in her right hand. The blade was thick. It looked as if it had been carved from stone. The handle looked like the withered branch of a tree, the bark coarse and bumpy.

The followers formed a queue before Helen. First in line was the woman with the perm. She stood before Helen, her left hand outstretched, positioned above Helen's face.

Margaret took a hold of Helen's hair and pulled, tipping her head back so that she was now staring at the ceiling. "Your loyalty will be rewarded, my dear," Margaret told the naked woman before her. The woman nodded. Margaret then placed the blade of her knife against the woman's palm and sliced.

The blood flowed immediately, pouring from the woman's hand, splattering onto Helen's face. "Open wide," said Margaret, tugging at

Helen's hair once more. Helen could taste the blood, seeping into her mouth, filling her nostrils, sliding down her throat. She tried to fight, tried to pull away, tried not to swallow, but she was too weak; Margaret's grip on her hair remained firm. Her stomach twisted itself into knots, desperate to regurgitate the fluids that now filled her belly.

The woman bowed her head, a symbol of gratitude, then stepped aside, allowing the tall black man to take her place. He too held his hand out above Helen's face. "Your loyalty will be rewarded, my dear," Margaret repeated, before slicing open the man's hand. Again, blood poured from the wound, coating Helen's face, slipping down to the back of her throat. Helen squeezed her mouth shut tight, but Margaret reached around and dug her fingers into her cheeks, her fingertips burrowing into the flesh like the claws of a bird. Blood seeped over Helen's lips. She felt the vomit creeping up from her stomach, a bitter taste on her tongue. She held it back, managed not to puke.

Another man approached. He was young and athletic, the muscles rippling across his chiselled chest. His arms were thick and lined with veins – veins that were no doubt full of warm, sticky blood.

Again, Margaret sliced open his palm, the gore squirting from the wound and spattering over Helen's face, entering her mouth, filling her belly. Helen tried to spit out as much of the blood as possible, but there was no way for her to prevent the vast majority from slipping down her oesophagus.

This continued, with each member of the congregation approaching, naked, thanking Margaret as she sliced a wide gash into the palm of their hand. A thick mask of blood plastered Helen's face. She stopped fighting now, having quickly discovered that it was of no use. There was no escape. Whatever Margaret wanted to do to her, she'd just have to sit there and take it. And right now, what Margaret seemingly wanted was for her entire body to be painted in gore, slathered with the blood of these strangers.

Mark's parents approached. Like the others, both were cut, bleeding into Helen's mouth. Before she turned away, Mark's mother — Helen wasn't sure of her name — crouched before her. "Mark was a good boy," she growled, her voice low. "You may have taken his body from us, but his soul is with Satan now. He will live on forever."

When the last of them had bled onto Helen, their vital fluids having filled her mouth and seeped into her stomach, the crowd then stepped back, once again forming a circle around her. This time however, they joined hands, their blood mingling with that of their neighbour, dripping down into fibres of the filthy carpet.

Margaret pushed Helen forward, dropping her onto her face. "I'm afraid that it is your turn now," she said, crouching beside Helen. "But fear not – this will all be over soon enough. He is with us now."

Helen coughed out a thick wad of blood. "You're one crazy bitch, you know that?" she said, turning her head so that she could look up at Margaret. For the briefest of moments, Helen felt as if she wanted to burst out in fits of laughter. But then her stomach tightened, a crippling cramp constricting her innards.

Margaret was still smiling, unending, as if her withered lips had been drawn onto the blank canvas of her face. "You may *think* that I'm crazy," she said, barely able to contain her laughter. "But you are about to bear witness to the birth of the antichrist. Then you will see, I'm not crazy at all."

Pain surged through Helen's body. Her blood-filled stomach felt as if it were trying to fold itself inside out. It was like she could feel the thick bodily fluids of the followers churning around in her belly, bubbling away as if it were beginning to boil.

"He is coming!" said Margaret. "Hail Satan!"

"Hail Satan!" the followers echoed.

The pain in Helen's belly grew. There was something inside of her… something alive! She could feel it moving, writhing around inside her abdomen. Her stomach constricted, painfully squeezing against whatever this solid mass was that now resided within her.

What the fuck was this? How was this even possible?

She could feel something working its way up her oesophagus. But it wasn't vomit – whatever this was, it was hard and rigid. It choked her as it clawed its way up her throat. She pushed herself up onto her hands and knees, her back hunched like a cat, and coughed and spluttered, hoping to free herself of whatever this was now restricting her airways.

"He is with us! Rejoice!" Margaret bellowed excitedly.

"Hail Satan!" the followers repeated once more.

A bitter taste filled Helen's mouth, bile burning her tongue. Something foul and repugnant seemed to be burrowing through her internal organs, like whatever it was might just tear its way out of her chest, spilling her guts and splintering her ribs like in the movie *Alien*.

But movies were fiction – this was really happening!

The people around her were chanting now, their eyes closed, hands linked, blood smeared over their naked bodies, adhering to the folds of their flesh. Helen looked back to see that Margaret had now merged into the crowd, her own voice one with theirs.

Pain drilled through her body, the soft organic meat that made up her organs screaming out in agony. Something worked its way up her throat, much too large to fit. Helen could feel it, stretching the ligaments of her neck, pressing them outward as it squeezed along the narrow passage.

Helen finally retched, endless torrents of blood infused bile pouring from her gaping maw. Thick and black, the ichor filled her mouth and nose, preventing her from breathing. And then, dragged along by the cascading vomit, the large mass that had blocked her airways squeezed its way out, forced along by the waterfall of blood that spewed from Helen's gaping orifice.

It was over then. Helen collapsed to her front, a wave of exhaustion tearing her body out from under her.

The chanting of the followers ceased. An eerie silence befell the room.

Helen twisted her head to look at the puddle of gore she had produced just moments ago. There was something there, in it, alive. It squirmed and writhed in the blood.

Then it finally made its way to its feet.

--- --- --- --- --- --- --- --- --- --- --- ---

God is good. He has granted us life on this earth. He offers us salvation, whilst asking for very little in return. Yet, many of us still fall for the temptations of the Devil. He wishes to lead us into a life of sin. These vile horror movies are just a steppingstone on the pathway to hell. And although you may believe that to be a little over-dramatic, I can assure you, it is not. You may think that there is nothing to fear, but that is not true. There is much to fear. We should all be very afraid.

Margret Whitehead, conservative activist and author of 'Violence On Video: The End Of Morality?'

Chapter Fifteen:

Night Of The Demon

"Rejoice, my children!" said Margaret, stepping forth from the crowd, her hands raised above her head. "Our Lord is reborn!"

Helen couldn't believe her eyes. The thing before her in the puddle of gore looked like some sort of grotesque octopus. It looked like its entire body was made of muscle, black fibres contracting and relaxing in a repetitious manner. Blood dripped from the numerous limbs, onto which it now lifted itself. It seemed to have at least six legs, much like an insect. It held another four limbs limp and awkward before its body. Its thin, rat-like tail wavered slowly from side to side. Its head was much like that of a human baby, although it seemingly had no nose, and its mouth was much too wide; a gaping maw filled with a thousand needle-sharp teeth. It had black eyes and two bony protrusions on the top of its head – what Helen could only go so far as to describe as horns.

Trepidation seemed to fill the air, as if the people in there with Helen weren't actually sure what they were looking at. Helen considered the fact that maybe these people hadn't actually believed in what they were doing. But their faith had won out, and now they were staring at some demonic creature, the grotesque birth of which had been solely of their making.

"Hail Satan!" said one of the men in the crowd.

Satan? Is that what this was? Helen had never believed in such things. But now she was staring at the undeniable evidence of the existence of otherworldly creatures. As far as she knew, it was entirely possible that this thing — the thing that had just clawed its way out of her stomach — really *was* Satan.

The trepidation amongst the followers soon faded, replaced by a sense of joy. The followers were smiling, maniacal grins stretching their respective lips, their eyes black and full of lustful evil.

The demon snarled, a guttural, inhuman sound leaking from the back of its throat, almost as if it were choking. It hunched over, vertebrae protruding from its curved, twisted spine. Quickly then, it scurried over to the decimated torso of David's carcass. For a moment, Helen thought that it was trying to consume it, but quickly she realised that it was actually burrowing into the hollowed-out flesh.

The followers continued to chant as the creature squirmed its way inside the eviscerated chest cavity, blood leaking out, slivers of torn flesh cast aside.

"Watch," Margaret whispered into Helen's ear, having knelt beside her broken, exhausted form on the living room floor. "Witness the birth of our true saviour. He will put an end to this false God that so many worship. He will scorch the earth, and we will reign beside Him, princes and princesses of this ruined reality."

Helen watched. Her eyes watered as if they were being burned with acid, a bitter stench of sulphur filtering up her nostrils. She felt sick, ready to vomit once more. But she wouldn't let it come; she feared for what else might exit her body.

She felt tired.

She felt as if she were slowly going insane.

The skin of David's abdomen rippled, then split. Thick, black tendrils began to snake from the craters that remained where the chainsaw had chewed through the corpse. Like roots spreading out from a virulent fungus, the bloody tendrils slithered across the carpet, searching for the parts of the body that had been removed. A cluster of black veins crawled from one of the shoulders like an insect, slowly creeping towards the arm nearest to it. There, the veins pushed their way in under the skin of the arm, roughly stitching the two pieces back together.

"Oh my God," Helen muttered, as each of the severed limbs was reattached to the body, tendrils running between each organic component. New limbs seemed to be sprouting from the torso too, where the skin had opened up. Long animal-like arms, with three-fingered hands, dragged their way out of their deceased human host, curved talons tearing through the carpet.

Margaret laughed. "Does this look like the work of God?" she asked.

Gory slivers of raw flesh expanded out from David's long-dead abdomen, each of the shoulders reattaching to the severed arms, the hips reattaching to the legs, spreading outward from the mound of meat from which this demonic entity seemed to be expanding. Then each joint that Margaret had destroyed seemed to rebuild itself, not as flesh and bone, but as slimy, pulsating masses of grey meat, veins squirming beneath the surface as if they had a mind of their own. The joints of the elbows and the wrists, the knees and the ankles, all stitched back together. The result was a corpse that looked as if it had been stretched on some medieval torture rack, the skin having split, blood and pus oozing from the exposed muscle beneath.

And then there was the head. The same tendrils snaked out of the neck and crawled their way into the two halves of David's bisected head. Those two halves also became re-joined, although the space between them was now home to another face; a dozen black eyes, a wide grin filled with shark-like teeth, two vertical slits where the nose should have been. A pair of twisted, goat-like horns protruded from the top of the skull.

Helen couldn't believe what she was seeing. She'd hoped that this might have been her imagination playing tricks on her, or that this was some kind of a nightmare – one from which she'd soon awaken. But there was no denying it now; this was all real. The demonic creature now standing before her — at least eight feet tall, assembled from the various parts of David's dismembered corpse — was really there.

And there seemed to be life in David's eyes. They were looking around the room, much further apart than they ever should have been, staring at the numerous people that surrounded them, examining them, trying to figure them out.

As before, the followers were staring at the beast – some vile amalgamation of David's dismantled carcass and some nightmarish hell monster. But that sense of joy they had once felt had seemingly faded. Now, many of them seemed to be downright terrified. And Helen could understand this entirely. Blood slid down those additional limbs that had sprouted from the chest of David's corpse, the thick black arms, skin pitted like the bark of a tree, that now maintained the creature's seemingly precarious upright position.

Margaret stepped forward. If she felt any of the fear that emanated from the others, she hid it well. "Our Lord," she said, her arms raised. "Praise be to you. We devote ourselves to you, to do as you command. Hail Satan!"

"Hail Satan…" the followers chorused, each of them now sounding much less sure of themselves.

The creature turned its head, looking over them. It didn't appear to understand the words that Margaret had spoken. It seemed to Helen that this thing before her was no more than an animal, albeit a grotesquely horrifying one, and not one of this earth. What it was, she didn't know, but she felt sure that this was not the devil Himself. What Margaret and her followers had forced Helen to birth was no more than some ungodly demon.

Margaret spoke once again. "Lord Satan! We are your puppets. We await your command. Do with us as you see fit. We are yours. Hail Satan!"

"Hail Sa…"

The creature took a step towards the followers, cutting off their repetitive chant before they'd even managed to form the words. The youngest of the women shuffled back, grasping onto the arm of her companion, shielding herself behind his shoulder.

The demon hissed, its teeth bared.

Helen could feel the panic growing amongst the followers. What had they expected? Was this not what they had wanted? She felt sure all of a sudden, that most of the people there hadn't genuinely believed in what they were doing. They hadn't believed the things that Margaret had told them. And now, as they saw this monster standing before them, slowly creeping its way towards them, they understood that they had been sadly mistaken.

What a bizarre sight they were. All those people standing there, completely naked, the blood spilled from the wounds in their palms smeared across their bodies. They looked like a group of deranged maniacs. Helen almost wanted to laugh.

Perhaps it was *she* who was truly deranged.

“Satan!” Margaret screamed, demanding that the creature turn its attention to her. “I stand before you as your loyal servant. Tell me what you want from me, I beg of you.”

The creature looked back over its shoulder, back to where Margaret was standing, her arms outstretched as if she wished to embrace the monster. But it was impossible to understand just what this thing was thinking. Its black eyes, clustered together like those of a spider, gave nothing away. David’s eyes seemed to hold a look of disdain, although Helen imagined this might have been due to the fact that it was Margaret who had killed him. He had seemingly given his life willingly, but perhaps in death, he now understood that his sacrifice had been for nothing.

“Come to me,” Margaret urged.

The creature ignored her. It turned its attention back to the terrified girl, sniffing at her as if the scent of her fear was the most glorious fragrance it had ever smelled.

She could hold back no longer…

The girl screamed.

The creature roared. It swiped at her with one of its many hands, the curved talons that tipped its fingers slicing through the flesh of her stomach, her innards sloughing out through the cavernous wound. Her life instantly snuffed, her eviscerated corpse slammed into the man beside her, knocking him back, causing him to trip over the edge of the sofa.

A cacophony of noise filled the room as more people began screaming, scrambling around, trying desperately to escape the clutches of this terrible thing they had created.

And with each scream that left the lungs of the followers, the beast matched them with an inhuman roar of its own.

"No!" yelled Margaret, frantically flapping her arms, hoping that this might somehow calm the situation unfolding. "Stop! This isn't right! Everybody needs to relax! Stop with all this noise!"

But nobody was listening.

Her bones aching, Helen used her hands and her feet to push herself backwards, into the corner of the room. From there, she watched as the creature grabbed the farmer in two of its hands and bit into the side of his neck, the wound so deep that his head was now barely attached to his shoulders, no more than a sliver of flesh holding it in place. Another of the followers tried to run from the room, but the beast caught her quickly, its claws digging into her back and tearing out her spine like one might debone a haddock.

"No!" screamed Margaret, once again. She grabbed a hold of the demon's wrist — one of those that had once belonged to David — and tugged, trying to pull it away from the victim it was currently devouring, as if she might be able to stop this madness somehow. "This isn't *supposed* to be happening! We are your *disciples*! We live only to serve *you*!"

The thing turned, ceasing its attack on the black man, dropping his limp carcass, the top of his head having been cracked open like a boiled egg, his brain leaking out like a perfectly cooked yolk.

"Please," Margaret begged, as the demonic entity turned to face her. "This has to stop. We are your loyal servants. You cannot do this to us."

The creature seemed to be staring into her eyes, searching for a soul that Helen felt sure didn't exist. And then, without warning, it plunged its hand into her stomach, its razor-sharp claws tearing through the soft flesh, her abdominal muscles offering no resistance. The creature then pushed its hand upward, beneath her ribs, into her chest cavity. Blood oozed over Margaret's lips.

When the thing tore its hand free, it pulled loose a cluster of Margaret's viscera, her lungs and her heart pouring from the savage wound in a cascade of gore.

By the time Margaret's corpse hit the floor, the rest of the followers had fled. Only Helen remained in the farmhouse living room with this unearthly creature. Slowly, it stalked towards her. Helen wanted to close her eyes and pray that this might be over quickly. But then her eyes fell onto the chainsaw that Margaret had dropped earlier. It was right there, by her feet. She just needed to hook the toe of her shoe under the handle, then she might be able to pull it toward herself.

The creature was already bearing down on her though. A wide hand, with its slender fingers, wrapped around Helen's neck. The skin was as rough as sandpaper, like its palms were entirely calloused. And it smelled awful, a pungent odour of rotting flesh and sulphur emanating from its body. As it lifted her from the floor, its petrifying eyes locked onto her own, it didn't see — nor would it understand — the power tool she now held in her hands. Not even as she pulled the chainsaw's starter cord and the engine roared to life did it seem to understand what was coming next.

Helen gritted her teeth. She raised the chainsaw, directing the blade between the monster's legs. The teeth chewed through the creature's black flesh and the flesh of David's necrotic carcass alike, deep into its abdomen.

The demon roared as the chainsaw quickly carved through its body. It released its grip on Helen, sending her tumbling back down to the floor. For a moment, the saw remained fixed in place, hacking away at the creature's flesh and bone, until so much of the meat had been decimated, that it tore free, falling to the floor and stalling on impact.

The mewling beast seemed to be in pain. Dark green blood and mangled meat cascaded from its body like a waterfall. Weakened now, it stumbled around the room, knocking furniture aside, clawing at the walls, trying desperately to keep itself upright. But its attempts were futile; it stumbled backwards, howling as it crashed into the fireplace, sending burning logs and fiery embers scattering around the room.

The nylon fibres of the carpet began to melt first, before catching on fire. The sofa was aflame then, as were the curtains.

Agony racking her body, Helen knew she needed to move. If she didn't, she was dead. She rolled to her front and began to crawl towards the door.

Flames licked at the ceiling, melting the paintwork, blackening the exposed timbers that supported the floor above. It was the creaking and cracking and snapping of the wood above her head that urged Helen onward. A searing pain burning in her limbs, she pushed herself up to her feet and lurched her way out of the inferno, out into the hallway beyond. There, she pinballed from wall to wall, forcing herself along until she reached the front door. Out onto the porch, she stumbled down the steps, her feet giving way beneath her once more, sending her crashing to the dirt.

Her entire body ached. She rolled to her back and stared up to the sky above. She breathed deeply, enjoying the cool air that filled her lungs.

When she finally looked back to the house, the first thing that caught her eye was the jack-o'-lantern, still sitting on the doorstep, reminding her that it was, in fact, still Halloween night. It was grinning at her, as if it knew a secret, as if it had known all along what was happening to Helen inside that house, and as if it had somehow enjoyed the show.

But then that snarling pumpkin was smothered by the collapsing roof of the porch, the blaze having chewed through the front wall of the farmhouse. The rest of the house gave way soon after, crumbling into a heap of broken wood and plaster, the fire raging deep inside, a thick column of black smoke towering into the sky.

Helen collapsed to her back. Sleep overcame her as the fire continued to blaze, the corpse of the demon, and those of the dead followers, trapped beneath the burning rubble.

Burning, Helen thought, as the darkness invaded her. *Just as they deserved.*

--- --- --- --- --- --- --- --- --- --- --- ---

Monsters don't exist. They aren't real. People are the real monsters of this world. And I'm not even talking about serial killers and rapists. I'm talking about the politicians and the activists. We should be scared of what these people want to take away from us, the control they wish the exert over us. They don't want us to live our lives as we see fit. They want us to live the lives that they want. They want us to be the people that they deem necessary, or valuable to society, to serve their own twisted agendas. It's like a cult. It's those people who scare me. I can quite happily watch something like The House On The Edge Of The Park *and not even bat an eyelid. But these people... It's they who terrify me.*

Adam Chambers, independent

filmmaker and horror movie fanatic

Chapter Sixteen:

Exposé

Helen spent four days in the hospital, and she barely remembered a single second of it. Certainly not the first two days. During that time, she'd supposedly been in some kind of a coma, although her condition had never quite deteriorated to the point of being deemed critical.

Still, by the time she left, she had been given a catalogue of the injuries she had sustained. There were multiple lacerations, the worst of which had been to her left shoulder, and had required five stitches to close. She had been stabbed in the hand too, the blade of the implement her attacker had used having penetrated through, from one side to the other. Thankfully, none of her metacarpal bones were damaged, so the wound — currently wrapped in a thick layer of bandage — should heal quite nicely. Helen couldn't even recall when she may have sustained this wound. Nor did she know just when she had fractured her right ankle. Regardless of when it might've happened, the doctors had fixed it in place with a plaster cast.

She had broken two fingers on her left hand, and one on her right. She had a black eye, a broken nose, and a split in her lower lip. She also had a nasty kidney infection, which felt as if a thousand knives had been buried inside her chest cavity, pain searing her nerves with every breath. Worse still was the fever that this had afflicted her with.

This was no doubt due to the volume of blood she'd been forced to consume.

She hadn't told anybody about that though; not the doctors, nor the police. She hadn't even told her mother. What would be the point?

Nobody would believe her. They'd just think she was crazy – and understandably so. As such, when she spoke about what had happened to her, she decided against ever mentioning the ritual, or the demon.

The police had found more than a dozen bodies at the slaughterhouse, though. Many of them were people she didn't know. But her friends, of course, had been among them. They'd found Kevin's bloody corpse in his overturned car. Because of this, she'd at least had to tell them about what had happened to her, even if she was intentionally vague with the details.

She told them that she didn't know who any of the people were, and that she didn't know why they had done the things they did. She told them that the killer was one of them, and that Mark had been too, before his untimely demise. She told them that she had needed to fight her way free, and that she didn't know how the farmhouse had caught fire. She told them that she didn't know if anybody had escaped the house alive, before it had collapsed.

The police reassured Helen that they would do everything within their power to identify the members of the cult. In fact, they had already found a number of bodies within the wreckage of the collapsed house, and they hoped to positively identify them in the coming weeks.

Helen wondered whether or not they had found the body of the creature. Most likely not. If they had, then surely they'd have said something. She considered the possibility that perhaps the demon itself might've melted away, absorbed back into the Hell from which it came, leaving behind only David's dismantled cadaver.

The truth was, however, that whatever they found, Helen didn't really care. All she knew for sure was that, as soon as she was done with her studies, she'd be leaving Oakhill for good.

She might even try to convince her mother to come with her.

She'd never quite understood why her mother had insisted on staying for so long after George Milton's massacre all those years ago. Helen had asked her mother this very question on many occasions, and her answer had always remained the same – this place was her home. Well, as far as Helen was concerned, her home was wherever she felt happy and comfortable. Oakhill was not that place. She would be leaving as soon as possible.

Although she loved her mother, Helen just didn't want to end up like her. She didn't want to raise kids in this town, inflicting her own trauma on them.

Kids… Helen had never really thought about her future in that way. But she knew now that she wanted them someday. But she wouldn't allow them to grow up with a screw-up for a mother, like she had.

She *would* be a screw-up now though, wouldn't she? That was what had happened to her mother, and now they had more in common than they ever had before. If anything, Helen had suffered far more than her mother ever had…

But that was the future. So much was yet to happen. Helen wondered what the future might actually be like. She thought ahead twenty years. What would life be like then? Would much have changed? The movies seemed to suggest that there'd be flying cars by then, or that everybody would be living on the moon. Helen doubted that would be the case. But what about another twenty years after that? That would take them to 2024. She'd be on the verge of turning sixty. Surely so much would've changed by then. Would the world be a better place? Probably not. It'd probably be more like *Planet Of The Apes*; the entire human race completely fucked.

When the doctors finally discharged her and her mother came to pick her up, she insisted on pushing her around in a wheelchair. Helen could've gotten by on crutches, but she wasn't going to complain; she was in a lot of pain, and taking the weight of her one, un-broken foot offered her some much-needed relief.

A cool breeze was blowing outside. As her mother wheeled her across the car park, Helen found herself growing cold, an icy shiver running down her spine. But that was okay; it was better that the burning sensation she'd felt over the past few days, a symptom of the fever attacking her body.

Finally in the car, Helen's mother offered her a smile. She had tears forming in her eyes. "Okay," she said. "Let's get you home. Oh, God – you wouldn't believe how happy I am to finally be taking you home. I thought I'd lost you." One of those tears escaped the confines of her eyelid, and rolled down her cheek.

"You can't get rid of me that easily," said Helen, offering a smile of her own. She wasn't sure why, but she felt an amazing sense of joy swelling up inside her, so grateful to still be alive.

"I never want to let you out of my sight again," sniffled her mother.

Helen decided against telling her that she intended to leave town as soon as she possibly could. Instead, she just offered her another smile.

Her mother took her hand and squeezed it tightly. "How are you anyway? I mean, like, how are you, *really*?"

Helen nodded her head, fighting back her own tears. "I'm fine, Mom. Other than the severe pain I'm in, of course. But the medicine will take care of that, I'm sure. Honestly, you don't have to worry about me. I'm gonna be okay."

Her mother nodded, understanding. She turned the key in the ignition, firing up the car. "Alright," she said. "Let's get you home, back to some kind of normalcy."

Most of the journey home was taken in silence. Not until they neared the house did Helen's mother speak again. "I thought we could order pizza for dinner tonight; that new *Pizza Hut* just opened in town. How does that sound?"

Helen smiled, genuinely excited by the prospect. "That sounds great."

"And I thought maybe we could rent out a video to watch. Is there anything you fancy watching?"

Helen shook her head. "No. I'll happily watch anything, just so long as it's not horror."

"No video nasties then?"

Helen scoffed at the suggestion. "No, most definitely not. I hope they ban those godforsaken movies forever."

--- --- --- --- --- --- --- --- --- --- --- ---

Long live the video nasties!

Adam Chambers, independent
filmmaker and horror movie fanatic

THE END?

ABOUT THE AUTHOR

Harrison Phillips is an English author of extreme horror and splatterpunk fiction. His literary influences range from Clive Barker and Stephen King, to Jack Ketchum and Edward Lee. He enjoys playing video games and watching 70s/80s exploitation movies. He was born and raised in Birmingham, England, where he still resides with his long-suffering wife, their two daughters, and a schnauzer named Minnie.

ABOUT THE PUBLISHER/EDITOR

Dawn Shea is an author and half of the publishing team over at D&T Publishing. She lives with her family in Mississippi. Always an avid horror lover, she has moved forward with her dreams of writing and publishing those things she loves so much.

Follow her author page on Amazon for all publications she is featured in.

Follow D&T Publishing at their website, **www.dt-publishing.com**, or search for their Facebook Group

Or email here: dandtpublishing20@gmail.com

A Great British Video Nasty Nightmare by Harrison Phillips

Cover art by Don Noble

Edited by Tasha Schiedel

Formatted by Ash Ericmore

www.ingramcontent.com/pod-product-compliance
Lightning Source LLC
Chambersburg PA
CBHW051955220626
47052CB00004B/953
* 9 7 8 1 9 6 4 0 5 3 0 1 1 *